Clara was unaware of the decepetive plot.

"We're gonna get him a woman, that's what." Jude waited for their responses. . . . "We'll send a ticket to a woman in Norway."

"Hey, how you gonna get 'er name?"

"Easy, stupid. I jist happened to read the name and address offa that Detschman woman's letter to her baby sister."

"Oh." The men nodded in satisfaction. Trust Jude to think of something like that.

"Along with the ticket, we'll send a picture of me and a letter from Dag."

"He can't write no letter. He can't even read." Henry thumped a limp fist on the table top.

"I know that. But I can write—and read. The letter'll tell her about what a successful man he is—"

"He is that. Dag's the best blacksmith in six counties."

"Don't remind me! And it'll say how handsome—"

The men guffawed and slapped their knees.

"An' she'll expect to fall in love and marry him—" The laughter raised a decibal or two. . . .

" An' Dag'll 'bout die of embarrassment." Jude raised his refilled glass; the others followed suit. "To the end of Dag."

LAURAINE SNELLING is a full time writer who has several books published, including two other *Heartsong Presents* titles. *Song of Laughter,* which marked Snelling's debut as a *Heartsong Presents* author, won the Golden Heart award for excellence in fictional romance.

Books by Lauraine Snelling

HEARTSONG PRESENTS

HP10—Song of Laughter
HP28—Dakota Dawn

Dakota Dream

Lauraine Snelling

A sequel to *Dakota Dawn*

Heartsong Presents

*This book is dedicated to Inga, Thelma, and Clara,
my three favorite Norwegian sisters.*

My thanks to Reverend Steve Syverud, Doris and Bob Hendrickson, Harry Langenes, Thelma Sommerseth, Clara Rasmussen, and Gilbert Moe for sharing their heritage and memories. They say they didn't do much but I know different. If there are mistakes in this book, it surely isn't their fault but mine alone.

ISBN 1-55748-428-7

DAKOTA DREAM

prologue

To call Jude Weinlander a scoundrel was painting him with the brush of kindness. Bully and cheat were equal approbation. Blond, curly hair, blue eyes, the face of an angel but within his broad-shouldered physique lodged the soul of Lucifer himself. As for all of his ilk, his degree of impunity increased in direct proportion to the weakness of those he harassed.

He'd been hounding his brother Dag since Jude's first squall while in the cradle.

One night in 1910 when fall first nipped the Red River Valley of North Dakota, Jude and his bunch were slapping cards and slugging whiskey in their favorite haunt, Ole's Saloon.

"An' I'll raise ya two." Jude shoved his money toward the growing pile in the center of the green felt-covered table. He rocked back until his chair teetered on two legs, tapping the top of his cards with one finger. "Come on, Shorty. Make up your mind, we don't got all night."

"Na-a-a, too high for m' blood." Shorty threw down his cards and leaned forward so his shoulder blades stuck out of his shirt like wings, bird wings, definitely not those of angel type.

"Henry?" Jude tossed back the brown liquid in his glass and swiveled around to look for the bartender. He raised his glass. " 'Nother one, Ole. Whyn't ya just leave the bottle?"

"I'll play the next hand." Henry dumped his cards and reached for the bottle the bartender had left. His hand shook, sloshing the liquid over the edges of his glass. His high-pitched giggle belied the broad chest and ample girth.

"Ah-h, you're drunk." Jude fanned his cards again and squinted through the cigar smoke. His chair squalled in protest at the angle it was forced to maintain.

"I'll take that and call you." The dealer laid his cards face down on the table and pushed his money into the center. He turned his cards. "A flush."

"Hah!" Jude thumped his chair upright and spread his cards on the table. "Full house. Aces high." He reached out and pulled the pile of bills and change over. "Thank you, boys. Sure can use this extra cash. Ya done me a good turn, ya did."

He sucked in on his cigar and blew the smoke toward the ceiling. " 'Nother hand, just to see if'n ya can get some back?" He stared around at the five men gathered within the circle shed by the hanging gaslight.

"No?" He poured a shot into the glass at his elbow. "Don't say I didn't give ya all a chance." He set the bottle in the middle of the table where his stack of winnings had presided. "Have a little to warm ya on y'r way."

While the others poured and passed the bottle, Jude chuckled to himself. " 'Member I tol ya I had an ide-e?" At their nods he continued. "This'un's a real winner. Dag's gonna be so flummoxed he'll never show his face in Soldall again."

"What'er ya thinkin'?" Shorty leaned forward, his pencil-sharp elbows digging grooves in the green felt.

"We're gonna get him a woman, that's what." Jude waited for their responses. At the men's quizzical looks, he snorted. "What woman would look once at him, let alone twice? See, this here's how we'll do it." They all leaned close, shoulder to shoulder. "We'll send a ticket to a woman in Norway."

"Hey, how you gonna get 'er name?"

"Easy, stupid. I jist happened to read the name and address offa that Detschman woman's letter to her baby sister."

"Oh." The men nodded in admiration. Trust Jude to think of something like that.

"Along with that ticket, we'll send a picture of me and a letter from Dag."

"He can't write no letter. He can't even read." Henry thumped a limp fist on the table top.

"I know that. But I can write—and read. The letter'll tell her about what a successful man he is—"

"He is that. Dag's the best blacksmith in six counties."

"Don't remind me! An it'll say how handsome—"

The men guffawed and slapped their knees.

"An' she'll expect to fall in love and marry him—" The laughter raised a decibal or two. One chair screeched in protest when it's occupant shoved it backwards, laughing fit to split his britches.

"An' Dag'll 'bout die of embarrassment." Jude raised his refilled glass; the others followed suit. "To the end of Dag."

"The end of Dag."

one

The way lay long between Norway and America. Clara Johanson tapped the edge of her sister's letter against her teeth as she strode up the last hill before the home farm. While she glanced up at the newly snow-dusted peaks that rose in ever steeper ridges to the east, she failed to appreciated their grandeur this time. All she could think about was America. How would she get to America?

She leaned against a pine tree to catch her breath from the steep climb. Her sister, Nora, had written about how flat North Dakota stretched, about a plague of grasshoppers, two small motherless children, and a silent, German farmer who was stealing her heart away. But she hadn't been able to afford to send a ticket yet.

Clara removed her wool scarf from her head and smoothed her deep honey hair back into its combs. She shook her head and the waves of gold rippled like wheat across her shoulders. Even in the brisk wind off the fjords, moisture dotted her forehead from the climb.

A squirrel chattered in the branches above her.

"Yah, I know, I'm bothering you. But what would you do in my place?" She stared up through the soughing branches to locate her scolding audience. "Most of my friends are already married but me. . .for me there's no one." Pieces of pine cone dropped around her. She tightened her dark skirts around her knees and sank to the ground softened with pine needles.

"Maybe I should volunteer to the government to be an immigrant bride. You know the Norwegian government is sending marriageable women out to different parts of the world to the men who want families." More cone pieces dropped, one landing on her shoulder. "You don't think I'd make a good wife?"

The squirrel chattered. One answered it from another tree.

Clara caught a flash of red as her comrade leaped from a branch above her to the tree across the track. "Well, I hope you do. See, God, even the squirrels have mates." She shifted her conversation partner without missing a beat. "But I don't. You know I am well-trained to be a wife and mother. Just ask Mor. She started teaching me when I was but a babe."

She thought again of the letter from Nora. Her words spoke of such love between her and Carl Detschman. It hadn't been easy, in fact, Carl had nearly died, but the love shone now from her sister's pen. Oh, to love and be loved like that.

With one fingertip Clara traced a cross in the duff. "I know you have a plan for me. . .for my life. Please let it be in America." She dug the lines deeper. "I'm trying to be patient, really I am." Her sigh lifted and tickled the bows above her. Her prayer rode the sigh to the tree top, begged a ride on the wind, and wafted upward to her Father's ears.

"*Uffda!*" Dag Weinlander grunted from the force of the kick. "Enough!" He slapped the horse's gray rump with a heavy gloved hand, then wiped the sweat dripping from his brow. He leaned over, grasped the horse's rear off fetlock, and dragged the bent leg between his knees to rest on the platfrom created by his gripping knees.

"Dag?"

He ignored the familiar voice, instead checking the symmetry of the iron shoe.

A knee-length, split-leather divided apron protected his legs from the hot iron shoe that raised a tendril of burned-hoof smoke when he set the iron against the wall of the horse's hoof. With iron nails clenched between his lips blackened by the forge smoke and his muscles bulging, he raised the hammer and tapped each nail into position. Dag set the shoe and cramped the nails puncturing the outside of the hoof. With the easy strokes of long practice, he rasped each head down and formed the hoof even with the shoe.

With a grunt, he dropped the horse's rear leg and straightened up, one hand pressed against the small of his back. Only one more to go.

"Dag!" A hint of a whine laced the demanding tone.

"Yah?" Dag peered out from the locks straggling over his brow.

"You won't forget?" Dag's younger brother, Jude, leaned against the post.

"Said I'd meet her." Dag picked up the iron flat tongs and shoved the final shoe back into the glowing forge. After a couple of cranks on the blower, the iron glowed red then white-hot. He set it on edge on the anvil and, with the hammer, pounded more of a curve into the heels. Sparks flew, bright red and orange, against the dimness of the cavernous shop. He dunked the shoe into the slack tub, the heated iron spitting steam into the smokey air.

"And you'll drive her out to the Detschman farm." This time it was more an order than a question.

"Yah." Dag brushed an intrusive lock of hair from his eyes, using the back of his wrist. Sweat muddied with soot streaked across his cheek.

"Her name's Clara, Clara Johanson." Jude continued propping the center post.

Dag leaned into the ritual with the remaining hoof. The horse snorted and twitched his tail. "Hold 'im."

"Yah. Easy feller." Will, the young helper, gripped the halter more tightly and stroked the horse's arched neck.

The coarse tail hairs snagged on Dag's head and one caught him in the eye. He brushed it away and clamped the hoof more tightly between his knees. The tearing of the injured eye blurred the hoof for a moment or two.

"I'll be goin' on then." said Jude. " You'll take care of Ma?"

Dag nodded, mouth too full of nails to answer. Of course he'd take care of Ma. When hadn't he? Or rather, when had Jude? Surprised at the unaccustomed thoughts, Dag concentrated on finishing off the hoof. The pungent odors of horse manure, cut hooves, horse hide, and smoldering coal all welded together redolent of blacksmithing. He breathed it in like bellows himself, part and parcel of his life and livelihood.

He rechecked each hoof and, when he straightened his back and looked around, only he and Will remained.

"He left 'bout the time you last answered." Will slipped loose the rope tying the horse to the post. "Seemed in a powerful hurry." He led the horse out the door and toward the livery barn. "You gonna do the other?"

"Yah." Dag heard the two horses whicker to each other, the timeless greeting of friendly horses. Will's voice joined in.

Dag removed his glove and rubbed the back of his neck with fingers so deeply grimed they looked like walnut bark. They matched his neck. He hawked and spit, then kneaded his protesting back muscles with hamlike hands. Outside he could see the daylight dimming.

Will trotted up with the remaining horse and tied it to the hitching post located in the arched doorway of the shingled building.

The train would be in anytime now. Dag stared from the horse to the tree outside. Not enough time. He shook his head. Why'd Jude make such a fuss over his picking up that woman? She could wait till he finished. Johnson's team came first.

He bent to the job at hand.

"You gonna eat first?" Will asked after stabling the freshly shod horse.

"Nah. You go on."

"I can help you get the buggy ready." Will shifted from one foot to the other.

Dag shook his head. "Go eat."

The train whistle had come and gone long enough for the gaslight above the hotel entrance to be lit before Dag hung his apron on a nail. He shrugged into a black wool jacket, then brushed down his own bay mare. When her coat shone to prefection, he gently laid the harness across her back, careful to smooth every hair under the leather and adjust each snap and buckle. When he backed her into the shafts it was a contest to see which shown brighter, the horse or the buggy.

He kicked his boots against a post to knock off any clinging mud or manure and stepped into the leather-roofed buggy. Jude had said to take the buggy. Dag shook his head. If that woman had many trunks and such, the wagon would be better.

He picked up the reins and clucked to the mare. The sooner he got this chore done, the better. His stomach rumbled. By the time he drove the nearly one hour out to the Detschman farm and another hour back, his belly'd do more than rumble. He rubbed a hand over a wall of solid flesh. In the dim light he picked a clump of dirt—manure?—off his pant leg and flicked the matter out of the buggy.

His stomach grumbled again—louder.

He turned the mare in beside the weathered train station and stopped beside the raised platform between the hunching building and the ribbon tracks. Two trunks squatted side by side.

With a sound of disgust, Dag levered himself from the buggy. He should have brought the wagon. Now he'd have to make another trip tomorrow.

"*Uff da,*" he muttered as he knotted the mare's lead shank around the hitching post. Let Detschman come in and get 'em. She was his sister-in-law anyway, wasn't she? Why didn't he meet the train? That Jude—what'd he have to do with this whole mess anyway?

Dag stomped across the wide beaten planks and jerked open the door. It wasn't as if he had nothing else to do. And while Jude said he'd pay for the trip, getting the cash in hand was about as likely as a snowstorm in July.

"*Frøken* Johanson" The words died aborning. Dag tried to swallow but his mouth suddenly felt like a Dakota dust storm. That same storm left grit in his eyes. Was this what being struck by lightning felt like? Lightning didn't usually accompany dust storms.

He stared at the vision that stood before him. Tendrils of deep honey blond hair peeped out from the sides of a feathered black hat. Eyes the blue-green of a humming-bird's back peeked out from the black veil pinned in a swoop across an alabaster forehead. Turned up nose, lips ruby like the hummingbird's throat and smiling as if they'd been friends for years. When she stood, she barely came up to the middle button on his faded and tattered shirt.

Dag tried again to talk. Breathing alone took an effort. Both failed.

"I'm Clara Johanson." Her voice tickled his ears that responded in a rush of heat.

Dag wet his lips, or tried to. Spit dried in a dust storm. "And you're...?"

When had the Norwegian language been set to melody? He ordered his gaze to leave her face. To look up at the rafters or down at the floor. Instead, rebellious gaze. It traveled her length, from tip of crushable hat to toe of shiny boots—and back up. Now his ears burned like the forge he'd left behind.

Dag leaned forward and picked up the bag set beside her. He waved his hand toward the door and strode out in silence. He who rarely chose to speak, now couldn't.

He slung her gray-and-black bag into the small space behind the seat and climbed into the buggy.

"What about my trunks?" Clara paused at the edge of the station platform.

"Tomorrow." Dag croaked out the word.

Clara climbed into the buggy and settled her skirts. What a strange man. Maybe he was a bit on the deaf side? She sniffed, her nostrils pinching against the odor. Did he never bathe? Or wash that rat's nest of hair? She tried to ignore the fumes. Thank the good Lord above this wasn't the man in her picture.

She clasped her purse in her lap, wishing the buggy were even a few inches wider. She shifted as far to the side as possible.

"Nice evening, isn't it?" Maybe if she breathed through her mouth it would be easier.

Silence from the man beside her. The harness jingled with the trotting horse.

Clara peered ahead. Yah, like Nora had written, the land certainly was flat. A little bounce of excitement slipped past her mother's orders to act like the woman she now was... or would be. The time sequence wasn't exactly clear as to when a person left the exuberance of childhood and entered staid adulthood. She sneaked a glance at the man driving the buggy.

He stared straight ahead. Good. Mayhap he hadn't noticed. If only he hadn't taken so long to come for her.

Now it was too dark to see the fields and farms. Off to the right a light from someone's house pinpointed in the darkness.

The mare trotted onward, her puffs of breath a counterpoint to the tattoo of her hooves.

"What did you say your name is?" Her willful stubbornness kicked in. She *would* get him to talk. How could anyone be so rude?

"Have you lived here a long time?" She waited for an answer that didn't come. "Do you know my sister, Nora?" Waiting was getting harder. She wanted to ask him about the handsome man with curly blond hair, the one whose face she'd fallen in love with. The man who sent her a ticket and would be looking forward to claiming her as his wife. But she didn't.

"How far from town do Nora and Carl live?" Pause again. Clara felt like grabbing the man by the ears and turning his face to look at her so he would be forced to answer. "I know you speak Norwegian, I heard you. So I must take it that you are a cruel person at heart who is enjoying my discomfort. Newcomers to America like me must be most entertaining to ignore."

Was that a snort she heard? From the horse? No. Clara ran her tongue over her teeth and tipped her chin a bit higher. "Maybe you just want to hear me prattle away so you can tell all your friends what a simpering fool that new arrival is?"

"Uff da."

Clara nearly clapped her hands in delight. "I agree. No one should be forced to carry on as I have just to get two syllables from her driver."

"Dag. I am Dag Weinlander." How he had fought to ignore her jabs. Dag bit his lip to keep from laughing aloud. What a feisty little thing she was.

"I'm pleased to meet you, Dag Weinlander." Clara settled back against the leather seat. She'd won—the first round. Her forehead wrinkled. What a curious thought. Why should she think there would be other rounds?

Dag focused on the spot up the road between his mare's ears so that his errant gaze wouldn't turn to hers. The tips of his ears still burned or burned again, he couldn't say which.

What did she want from him? He'd been hired to drive her out to her sister's, not entertain her on the way. Once his ears stopped burning, they'd probably drop off from sheer over exertion. No one but Will had talked to him that much since. . .since. . .well, maybe they never had.

The clop of hooves, the jangling of the harness, and the creak of the iron-clad wheels sang through the dark.

Clara nibbled her lip. As long as she turned her face slightly to the side, she could breath the crisp night air, unimpeded by the odor of the man next to her. Her nose told her there would be frost before morning.

Ahead, a brass disc peeped its edge above the rim of the

earth. As the moon rose, it seemed to fill the eastern horizon with gold.

"Oh-h-h." Her wonder escaped on a sigh. With no mountains or trees to break it's symmetry, the moon took possession of the land, rising to float against the black vault of the heavens, bathing the earth in liquid light. Clara forgot the man beside her, her sister in the home awaiting her, and the family she'd left behind. She lost herself in the glory of the harvest moon, the brisk air that kisssed her opened lips, and the hush that blanketed all the simple sounds around her. "*Mange takk*, dear God." She whispered, sensing that anything louder might shatter the glory.

A crystal tear slipped down her cheek, mute testimony to God's nighttime handiwork.

Dag watched the girl beside him. He'd seen a harvest moon before and he'd felt its power and majesty. He'd never seen a woman bathed in moonglow and transfixed by it's beauty.

Clara shivered and took a deep breath. She looked around, as if surprised at her reaction. Her glance caught the movement of Dag's head from the corner of her eye. Had he been watching her?

Dag pulled gently on the left rein and turned his mare into the lane leading to the Detschman farm. "We're here."

Clare perched on the edge of the seat, straining to catch

the first glimpse of welcoming windows.

Ahead, lighted windows dimmed in the brightness of the moon. While leafless tress shielded the house, the moon reflected off the roof of a large barn, windmill, and various other buildings, all crouching against the earth's breast.

A dog barked. A horse whinnied from the pasture. The mare lifted her nose and answered.

A door opened, spilling light across the porch and down the steps.

Clara felt the tears gather and clog in her throat. She'd finally reached her sister's new home. Nora's American home. Now they'd be together again.

Before the buggy stopped rocking, Clara leaped from her seat and scrambled down the step to land lightly on the ground. She darted through the gate, up the walk, bounded the two steps while pulling up her long skirt, and threw herself into her older sister's arms.

"Clara, you're here already." Nora hugged her little sister close. "We didn't expect you until tomorrow or the next day."

"I wanted to surprise you." Clara leaned her head against her sister's shoulder. "I have so much to tell you." She wiped away an escaping tear. "I can't believe I'm here, in America, in North Dakota, with you."

Nora hugged her sister once more and then stepped back. "Clara, this is Carl." She took the hand of the man who waited patiently behind her and brought him forward.

"I am pleased to meet you." Carl extended his right hand, the left still clasped by Nora.

Clara nodded, her speech temporarily drowned by the tears she kept swallowing.

"And this is Kaaren." Nora reached behind her to grasp the little girl's hand, hiding in her mother's skirts. "Kaaren, your Auntie Clara from Norway."

Kaaren, finger in her mouth, buried her face in Nora's white apron.

Clara squatted down and looked the little one in the eye. "Oh, my. Now I'm an auntie. And you're my first niece. We're going to have such fun." She stood again.

"And where is that baby boy I've read so much about?"

"Sound asleep and we want him to stay that way. You can cuddle him tomorrow. Come in now."

"Oh, my bags."

"I'll get them." Carl stepped off the porch and headed for the buggy where Dag waited, patiently leaning against the high wheel.

As the sisters turned toward the warmth of the open door, Clara spun back around. "I haven't thanked Dag for bringing me all the way out here."

"Don't worry, Carl will take care of that for you. Have you had anything to eat? I'll make fresh coffee." They passed into the house.

Dag turned down Carl's offer of coffee and food and, after shaking hands, stepped back into the buggy. He touched a finger to his hat brim, turned the mare in a circle to head back out the lane, and clucked her into a trot.

He listened for the familiar night sounds. How faint they seemed after the chatter that had filled his ears. He'd never realized before how quiet the night could be. And how far away his hovel stood. He ignored the temptation to look back at the lighted windows.

two

"How then did you get the ticket to come?" Nora asked.

Carl had put Kaaren to bed and gone upstairs himself after wishing the visitor a good night's rest. Nora and Clara were enjoying a second cup of coffee in the now quiet and peaceful kitchen.

"I'll tell you. Let me get the letter." Clara slipped from her chair at the kitchen table and crossed the room to rummage in her suitcase. When she returned she held a water-stained envelope in her hand. "Here." She laid it on the table in front of her sister.

Nora studied the front of the envelope. She pulled the kerosene lamp closer so she could read the faded handwriting. After carefully studying it, she looked up. "How did this get so stained?"

"I don't know. It happened before—"

"Before you got it?" Nora's voice squeaked in amazement. She didn't pay attention to the fact that they'd fallen back in their old pattern of finishing one another's thoughts.

Clara nodded.

"Then how—"

"Did I get it?"

24

Nora nodded this time. Silence but for the clunk of a piece of coal falling in the stove waited while she studied the barely discernible script again. She looked up.

"I know. God must have had His hand in this—or else He just gave the postman extra good eyesight."

"*Uff da*." Nora shook her head again.

"Open it." Clara gave a little bounce on her chair. "Read the letter."

Nora grasped the fragile paper and pulled it from the envelope. After unfolding it, she choked back a laugh. "Was it really this bad?" She scanned the lines and loops of script; most of the ink had run together or faded entirely. She peered closely where the signature should be. "Impossible. All I can read for sure is 'Dear Miss Johanson.' At least I assume that's what the heading says."

"Me, too. But the ticket was plain enough to use— barely—and then there was this." She handed Nora a picture, faded in places, but still clear enough to see. "Isn't he handsome? Just think that's the man who sent me a ticket. Do you know him?"

Nora studied the picture. She glanced up at her sister and then went back to studying the photograph. "If he's as nice as he is good looking—"

"I know. I think I'm half in love with him already." Clara plucked the picture from her sister's hand and sighed when she gazed at the face of her mystery man. "Such hair, curly like that. And look, I think if he smiled, he would have a dimple." She touched the paper cheek with her finger tip. "You didn't say. Do you know who he is? I wonder why he didn't meet the train?"

"No, I don't. I mean I've never seen him before but then there are many people in Soldall that I've never seen. If they don't go to church. . . ."

"Surely he must go to church." Clara could feel her heart begin an erratic thump in her chest. "You really don't know him?"

Nora shook her head. She reached for her sister's hands. "No, but mayhap Carl does. Or Ingeborge." She covered both of Clara's hands with her own. "This is surely a mystery, isn't it? She picked up her coffee cup and sipped. "Ugh." The face she made accompanied the words. "Cold coffee. Let me warm yours up, too." She started to push back her chair.

"No, not for me." Clara stared at the picture, worrying her bottom lip between her teeth. Should she tell Nora about the little knot of fear that seemed to be cutting off her air? She sucked in a deep breath. A yawn caught it and creaked her jawbone.

"*Uff da*. Here we sit yakking when you just got off the train. I can see you need your bed. We can figure all this out in the morning." Nora tucked a strand of hair behind Clara's ear and caught her own yawn. "You made me yawn, too."

The clock chimed. . .and chimed.

"There, it is ten o'clock already and we've been sitting here for hours. Come. Carl brought Kaaren into my bed so you can have her bedroom. That way you can sleep as long as you want in the morning." Nora rose to her feet and laid a hand on her sister's shoulder. "Not to worry, little sister of my heart. Your man will show up one day and then you can decide if you like him as much as you think."

"Yah, that is the way of it." Clara stood, slipping the letter and picture back in the envelope at the same time. "I just thought you would know him and this would all be cleared up at once." She tapped the edge of the envelope with her finger.

"And tomorrow you can tell me all the news of home—"

"And give you the presents Mor sent and the letters, too. Everyone wrote when they knew I was to come." Clara lifted her chair so it wouldn't creak on the floor and snugged it up against the table.

Nora picked up the carpetbag with one hand and lamp in the other and led the way through the parlor to the back bedroom. She set the lamp on the oak chest of drawers and the bag in front. A rag doll flopped against the pillow covered by a patchwork quilt on the bed.

Clara sank down on the edge of the bed. "It seems like weeks since I've slept in a real bed." She picked up the doll and studied the black button eyes and smiling mouth embroidered in red. "This looks like your handiwork.

Remember the one you made for me?"

Nora nodded. "That was my first. And you pulled the eyes off in the first hour. After the second time I had to resew them, I embroidered the eyes, too, in green to match yours."

Clara laughed and gave the doll a squeeze. "You are very good with a needle. All the hardanger lace for your bride's chest. I had a hard time learning to sit still for so long. Mor did her best. Such patience she has."

Nora sat beside her sister. "And your bride's chest? Did you fill it?"

Clara nodded. "But just don't look too close at the stitches. Oh, I forgot. My trunks are still at the station. Mr. Weinlander said Carl would have to come get them since he had only the buggy."

"How did he know to meet you?"

Clara blinked. She looked to her sister. "Why, I don't know. I never thought of it. The stationmaster told me the man from the livery would come for me. I waited quite a time and when he finally came—*uff da*." She wrinkled her nose. "I don't think he's ever heard of a bath, let alone taken one. And rude." She planted her fists on her hips. "Getting him to speak was—"

Nora chuckled. "And did you? Get him to talk?"

"But, naturally." Clara flopped back on the bed, looking at her sister as if she'd doubted the sun would rise.

Nora shook her head. "Dag just doesn't talk to anyone.

He says the fewest words possible to complete his business. And that's all."

"Oh." The little word carried a wealth of understanding. Clara chewed the inside of her lower lip. She felt the chuckle dance around the corridors of her mind before bursting forth full-blown; it's merry music skipped from bed to window and around the room.

Nora shook her head. "What are you up to now, sister mine. I know that laugh."

Clara smothered her face with the rag doll. "Nora, dear, the man needs help."

"You just think about your mystery man. When you find him, you won't have time to be fixing Mr. Weinlander." She rose to her feet. "Now you sleep as long as you'd like in the morning. I know you're tired from the long journey and the bed will feel good." She reached out a hand to pull her sister to her feet. "Mayhap Carl can drive to town tomorrow for your trunks. And to tell Reverend Moen we can have the wedding Sunday. We were waiting for you, you know."

"But you're already married."

"I know. But that one seems a sham so we decided to have a real wedding, in the church and with me wearing my *bunad* and *sølje*. And with you to stand up for me once we heard you were coming."

"I am happy for you." Clara patted a hand over her mouth to disguise the yawn. "I'll see you in the morning then."

Nora folded back the covers. "I'll leave this lamp with you." She stopped again in the door frame. "You'll never know how glad I am you are here. Sleep well, God bless."

Clara stifled a yawn again. "*Mange takk*, dear sister." Her eyelids seemed weighted with stones as she removed her clothing and pulled her nightgown over her head. "*Mange takk*," was all she finished of her prayers before sleep winged her away to dream of a curly haired man with broad shoulders and the promise of a dimple in his right cheek when he smiled.

Clara awoke to silence. Where had everyone gone? She lay in the soft featherbed reviewing the hours spent on the train, back to the ship, and ended up at her parents' home in Norway. Such a distant place. Would she ever see the rest of her family again?

She bit the inside of her lip against the pain of missing them all. "Not all, silly. Nora's around here somewhere. Think how much you've wanted to see her and now you can." She threw back the hand-stitched quilt and sat up cross-legged in the bed. With her elbows propped on her knees, she rested her chin in her hands.

A song trickled through her mind, one learned in the choir at home. She hummed the tune while studying the white fabric stretched across her knees. The words came to her mind: *Oh God our help in ages past.* "Good thing." She left the tune and turned to prayer, clenching her eyes shut so she wouldn't be distracted by the sun's painting squares on the polished floorboards. "Father God, I know You've always been with me and this journey proved Your faithfulness again. But what about the man who sent for me? Where is he? Who is he? How can I marry him if . . .if. . . ." She waited for her thoughts to settle down. "I do so want to be married. I know I make jokes about it but, Father, I need someone to love. . .someone who loves me. I want a home and a family." She paused again. A far off *moooo* blessed her silence. "Is that wrong of me?" No answer floated down from the heavens. None arose from her heart either.

A sigh rose from deep in her heart. It was hard to wait for an answer. She quieted her mind again. The song returned, the pace faster, the notes livelier. Unable to resist the joy she felt rising from somewhere deep inside, she whispered a final "Amen," and flung herself back on the pillows.

She stared up at the high ceiling, then wrapped both hands around her shoulders and squeezed. "I, Clara Johanson, am now in America!" She jumped from the bed, danced on the rug, and then got dressed. While the sun was shining in so warmly, the room felt like a cold fall day after a frosty fall night.

The clock bonged nine times as she opened her bedroom door and walked through the parlor toward the kitchen. While the house was empty, the coffeepot steamed gently on the back of the stove.

"Bless you, sister mine." She poured herself a cup and, wrapping both hands around the warmth, basked in the heat of the stove. As her gaze wandered around the kitchen, admiring her sister's handiwork, she stopped at the loaf of bread resting on the counter beside the jam jar and the molded butter on a plate.

She left her place at the stove and stuck a finger in the jam and then into her mouth. "Ummm." She licked all the sticky sweet berry taste off her finger and, after setting down the coffee cup, sliced herself a piece of bread. After burying it in butter and jam, she took the bread and coffee and eased herself down into the smaller of the two rockers in front of the stove.

"Ahhh." Alternately drinking and chewing, she continued her study of the kitchen. The stove had been recently cleaned and its silver trim gleamed in the beam of sun from the window. The ruffled curtains that framed the picture perfect fall tree in the window above the sink sparkled in the same sun. Clara nodded. Yes, her sister was the spotless homemaker their mother had trained her to be. . . always the one to be perfect at what she did.

Clara set the chair to rocking with the tip of her toe. Well, at least her hardanger stitching always outdid her sister's. She sighed and leaned her head against the back of the rocker. It was always hard to measure herself against perfection, yet she loved her older sister as only a younger one can.

"I've missed you so," she whispered to the tune of the clock chiming the hour. She plunked her feet on the floor and pushed herself to her feet. "And I've had enough of this lazing around. Nora, dear one, where are you? And those precious children of yours." She set her cup in the sink, covered the bread, and pushed the coffeepot to the side of the stove.

She lifted her coat from the hook on the rack and stepped outside to a glorious day of sun that warmed her cheeks. A fall-nipped breeze lifted the golden tendrils curling about her face. *Maybe today will be the day,* she thought, *the day my curly haired man will come riding up the lane.* She stared up the empty lane with two lines of hard-packed soil the width of wagon wheels. A line of grass grew in the middle.

"Clara, down here." Nora waved from the low building to the side of the barn.

Shrugging off the dream, Clara waved back and, leaping from the porch, trotted down the path. The windmill creaked it's song and, when she looked up, she saw a *V* of geese heading south, adding their wild cries to the plaintive notes of the windmill.

"You can carry the eggs," Nora said, her smile wide and eyes dancing, "or Peder." She motioned to the baby slung in a scarf and riding on her hip.

Kaaren, finger in her mouth, peeked from behind Nora's

dark wool skirt. Her coffee-colored hat had tilted slightly to the side, nearly hiding one blue eye.

Clara squatted down, eye level with the shy little girl, and crossed her arms on her knees. "I'm your Auntie Clara, remember?"

Kaaren nodded, her finger stuck firmly in place.

Clara itched to reach out and straighten the hat but she could remember being the shy one. "Maybe you could show me the cows and horses."

"Pa's cows." The finger left her mouth and pointed off to the barn. "Horses gone."

"Shall we go see?" Clara raised back to her feet and extended a hand.

Kaaren studied the hand and then looked up at Nora, as if asking approval. Nora nodded.

Kaaren reached out and slipped her hand in Clara's. When they started off, she hung back. "Ma come, too?"

Nora shook her head, her smile a benediction. She adjusted the baby's sling and picked up the basket of eggs. "You two go on. We'll have coffee when you come up to the house."

"I'll take those." Clara nodded at the egg basket. "After we see the cows."

Nora shook her head and started up the path.

Hand in hand, Clara and Kaaren meandered from the watering trough where the cows stood head to swishing tail, to the pen where the big black-and-white sow came to beg for bits of grass, to the corral where the work team dozed in the sun.

"Your pa is a good farmer," Clara said, admiring the tight fences and healthy looking livestock.

"Pa's gone to town." The finger went back into the little girl's mouth. Kaaren switched from English to German to Norwegian, depending on whatever word she wanted.

"Let's run." Clara tugged on her hand. Together, the two of them dashed up the path, through the gate, and bounded up the porch steps, Clara lifting her by-now-giggling-charge up the three stairs. She swung the little girl up in her arms and whirled her around before hugging her close and kissing her rosy cheek. "You're good enough to eat." Clara nibbled on the squirming little girl's neck.

Laughing and giggling they entered the house and removed their coats. When Clara picked Kaaren up so she could hang up her wrap, the little girl wrapped one arm around her aunt's neck after placing her coat on the hook.

"I see you've made friends." Nora set a plate of cookies on the table. "Wash your hands while I pour the coffee." She shifted the baby in her arm to the other side. He grinned and waved a chubby hand when Clara chucked him under his double chin.

With each holding a child on her lap, the two sisters dunked their cookies in their coffee and smiled at each other across the checkered red-and-white oilcloth table cover.

"I wasn't sure this would ever happen." Nora's look encompassed the entire scene.

"I know." Clara held her coffee cup steady while Kaaren dunked her cookie, too. "If it hadn't been for that letter, who knows how long."

"Surely Carl will know who it is when he comes back. He went in to talk with Reverend Moen about having our wedding on Sunday right after services."

"How will you get ready?"

"There's not so much." A pink tinge brightened her cheeks. "Oh, Clara, he—my Carl—he is such a good man. God is surely good to me."

"And to him. Look how you have cared for his children and—"

"But he had much sadness."

A silence fell and Clara reached out to cover her sister's hand with her own. "But now there will be much happiness. And I am here to make sure this marriage is done right. This time you will wear your *bunad* and sit for a portrait so we can send one home to Mor and Far.

"And maybe soon we will celebrate a wedding for you."

Clara shook her head. "When we find my mystery man. You don't suppose something has happened to him—"

"Like with my Hans you mean?"

Clara nodded. "To come so far like you did and your man had just died." She shuddered, as if a goose had just walked across her grave. "I don't know how you...." She shuddered again.

"As Mor says, 'We will give God the glory,' yah?"

"Yah, that we will." She rested her chin on the head of the little one against her breast. *And maybe one day, I'll have lambs like these,* Clara kept the thought in her heart. She had to find her man first.

When Carl returned from town he shook his head over the picture. "No, I don't know this man but maybe Reverend Moen will. He knows everyone for six townships."

"Or perhaps Ingeborge will?" Nora finished putting the last of the supper on the table. "Let's eat and you can tell all about your trip at the same time."

After bowing their heads for grace, Nora dished up the plates, set them in front of her family and then she sat down.

Carl turned to her, a twinkle in his eyes. "Reverend Moen said he'd be delighted to remarry us on Sunday since the first one didn't seem to take."

"Carl." Nora blushed and pushed at his arm. "You know that's not the reason."

He covered her hand with his. "So you say. And Ingeborge invited us all for dinner afterward."

"Did you ask her what we could bring?"

Carl nodded. "And she said 'Just yourselves.' This is to be her wedding gift to us." He took a bite of the pork chop smothered in applesauce on his plate. "Oh." He waved the fork for emphasis. "She said you are not to worry about a thing. New brides have too much on their minds already."

Clara watched the byplay between Carl and Nora. The tint creeping up her sister's neck was most becoming. How pleasant it was to watch someone get the better of her older sister. And to watch that someone do so with the lovelight shining so brightly in his own eyes, they needn't light the lamps. She felt a lump lodge in her throat.

"Auntie Clara."

"Yah, what is it?" She bent over to listen more closely to the whisper.

"Are you going to stay forever?" Kaaren stared up with eyes dark in the lamplight.

Clara felt the lump melt and begin to burn behind her eyelids. This little girl had already lost more than any child should when her mother died. "I don't know how long forever is but I plan on being around a long, long time." Her whisper seemed to be just what Kaaren needed to hear as the smile that brightened her face more than matched those exchanged by the two other adults at the table.

Kaaren's pigtails bobbed, she nodded so emphatically. "Good."

How long is long, Lord? Clara prayed that night after helping tuck Kaaren into bed and cleaning up the kitchen. Nora had set cooked cornmeal into loaf pans to fry for breakfast and started yeast rising for bread baking. How different it was watching her sister do the things their mother had always done. *Am I ready, Father?* Her prayer continued. *I know Your hand has been leading me but now . . .what has happened?* She shoved the niggling worries down and slammed a door on them. God wouldn't have brought her all the way to America without a purpose in mind. Would He?

But doubting was a sin. . .wasn't it? He did bring her . . .didn't He?

The thought of the man with curly hair flashed across her mind. Along with her mother's admonition, "Handsome is as handsome does." Clara had never understood what that meant.

The man was certainly handsome—wherever he was. Whoever he was. What should she do with the doubts? "Father, forgive me. Help me believe. . .and trust."

three

"In the name of the Father, and of the Son, and of the Holy Spirit, I now pronounce you man and wife." Reverend Moen closed his prayer book and nodded at the two standing before him. "Carl, you may kiss your bride." In an undertone, only for the ears of those four closest, he added, "Again."

Clara bit back a giggle. She could tell Carl and Nora had some ribbing in store for them since they had asked to be married a second time. But the teasing was such fun with the Moens.

The organ struck up the recessional. Clara handed her sister the white leather Bible with a small spray of gold and rust chrysanthemums on the top. Nora, clad in her black *skyjørt*, red vest, and white *forkle*, looked the perfect Norwegian bride even if she wasn't wearing the formal bridal headdress.

Clara reached up to kiss her sister's cheek. "God bless." She needed to wipe her eyes but her handkerchief lay in her bag, wherever that was. How come she always cried at weddings? It wasn't as if this were a sad occasion. She turned and followed Carl and Nora down the aisle.

Some members of the congregation had elected to remain to help wish the newlyweds God's blessing. Clara found herself searching the faces for a certain curly haired man but she hadn't found him by the time they all exited the sanctuary.

She hugged her sister again. "Oh, if only Mor and Far could have been here," Clara felt herself choke up again on the words. She wiped a tear from the corner of her eye.

"I know," Nora whispered back, "but at least you were here."

The pastor's wife, Ingeborge Moen, a baby in each arm and the other children clustered about her like chicks with a hen, herded her brood to the door.

"Here, let me take Peder." Clara reached out for the sleeping baby. She took the quilt-wrapped bundle carefully in her arms and, at the babe's whimper, slipped into the swaying motion common to women everywhere. She watched as Carl and Nora greeted the people around them.

"Such a wonderful story and with a happy ending," Ingeborge sighed at Clara's elbow. "Your sister is a fine woman. She has made Carl to laugh again."

"She never told us much about those early months." Clara patted Peder's back when he began squirming. "We had to read between the lines, more what she didn't say than what she did."

"It wasn't easy. Peder was colicky, Carl wanted her to speak only English and who was there to teach her and

Kaaren, poor mite, who missed her mother so bad. I tell you, those two earned their happiness."

Peder ignored the comforting sway and added his opinion to the discussion. As with all babies, his idea of communication after the first subtle whimpers that had been ignored, was a full-throated howl.

"Shush, shush." Clara jiggled harder.

The baby yelled—louder.

Clara looked around the room for the baby's mother. "They've gone into the office to sign the marriage certificate. Come." Ingeborge nodded to the outer door. "Let's take these two young ones home and feed them. And I have a marvelous idea." She picked up the conversation again after they'd corralled the older children running around outside and started down the street.

"Why don't you and the children stay with John and me tonight? Carl and Nora deserve to have a night alone, don't you think?"

"Why...why, I'm sure that is a fine idea, but do you have room?"

"Oh, there's always room for one more."

"Yah, but this is three and one of us isn't always the best company." She glanced to the baby whimpering in her arms.

"Did Nora tell you that I helped nurse Peder there for a few days?" Clara shook her head. "So that baby and I were pretty close for a time. We'd love to have him back and you can see how much Kaaren loves to be with Mary. You can have the same bed Nora used when she first came."

"If Carl and Nora agree, who am I to argue." Clara now knew what it must be like to be pushed along like a leaf on a spring freshet. How could you turn down a person who made everything look as if you were doing her a favor? And besides, who wouldn't want to be alone the first night? She felt a warmth creep up her neck. At least that's what folks said about newlyweds.

Clara didn't have time to think about the picture she had tucked away in her bag until after she and Ingeborge had kissed the children good night and listened to their prayers.

"What a wonderful day." She sank into one of the rocking chairs in front of the gleaming black-and-silver cookstove.

"Yah, I know those two will be truly happy. And did you see the blush on your sister's neck when we told her about you and the children staying here?" Ingeborge set the chair on it's creaking song with the toe of her foot. "Oh, to be so young again and beginning a life together."

Clara felt a tug in the region of her heart. She'd already pinpointed those twinges she'd identified as jealousy. Where was the man who had sent for her?

"I have something to show you." She leaned over and picked up her bag from the floor by the chair. She'd brought it back into the kitchen with her after kissing

Kaaren one last time. Surely Ingeborge would know who this curly haired dream man was.

With trembling fingers she opened the mouth of the black leather bag and pulled out the picture. "Here." She extended her hand across the space and handed the picture to Ingeborge. Why did her breath catch in her throat and her stomach feel like cream being tossed in a churn?

Ingeborge smiled her comforting smile and glanced down at the picture. "Yah, he is a fine looking man." She looked over at Clara with a question in her eyes. "Who is he?"

The churning in her midsection clumped together and fell to her toes. "I thought maybe you would know. This is the man who bought my ticket to America. He thinks he is getting a Norwegian wife but I've been waiting. He never appears."

"Oh, my." Ingeborge patted Clara's hand where it strangled the wooden arm of the rocker. She studied the portrait again, all the while shaking her head. "Oh, my dear, I wish I had good news for you." She paused. "But maybe John knows this man. I'll go ask him."

Clara leaned her head against the back of the rocker and let her eyes close after Ingeborge left the room. The memory of her mother's voice calmed her rampaging thoughts. Prayer was Mor's answer to anything and everything. But Mor, she wanted to plead, its been four days and I haven't heard from him. Like the kiss of butterfly wings, her mother's voice reminded, pray for him.

"That's not so easy," Clara muttered. "I don't know his name or anything about him." She could feel a smile tickle the sides of her mouth. But oh, he was beautiful.

She opened her eyes when she heard Ingeborge in the doorway. What was the look she caught on the woman's face? It had been so fleeting. Was it—no—she didn't get a chance to think about it again.

"John thinks the man looks familiar but. . .ahh. . .he isn't . . .he can't say he knows him either." She stuttered in an uncharacteristic fashion.

Doubts crowded into Clara's mind again. "Is there something wrong? Something you're not telling me?" She leaned forward in the chair, her hands clamped together in her lap. "Ingeborge, what is it?"

"Nothing, nothing at all. We. . .uh, John and I, we'll ask around." She turned to move the coffeepot over the hotter part of the stove. "John said he'll be in for a cup of coffee in a minute and then you can tell him the entire story." She crossed to the cupboard and took down the coffee cups.

Clara commanded that her hands unclench themselves while she took in a deep breath and let it out slowly. There *was* something they weren't telling her. There was. She could sense it.

But later when the three of them had taken their places at the table and munched crisp molasses cookies with their coffee, the feeling left. She told the entire story from the moment she first saw the water-stained and smudged envelope until the present.

"And you haven't seen anyone that looks like this man since you arrived?" Reverend Moen leaned forward in his chair.

"No. And not heard one word. It's as if he fell off the face of the earth." Clara took a sip of now cool coffee to quell the dryness in her throat. "Each day I think now this will be the time he comes forward but. . . ." She raised her hands, palm up in a gesture of resignation. She looked from the pastor to his wife. "He doesn't come."

Reverend Moen rubbed the bridge of his nose with one long finger. He nodded and looked up at her. "We shall see. We shall see."

That night in bed, Clara listened to the sounds of the house creaking and settling for the night. So far the only men she'd met in this new country had been Carl, Reverend Moen, and that blacksmith who carted her out to the Detschman farm. And none of them looked anything like the man in her picture.

A week later, when the weather dropped below freezing and hovered there even during the day, Carl announced they would begin butchering the next morning. All the young hogs were fattened and ready.

"Dag will be bringing out his scalding tank and helping me dip and scrape. I thought we'd give a side to the Moens." He glanced at Clara sitting at the other end of the table. "You ever raised pigs and butchered them?"

"Of course. Far and the boys did most of the work but I can grind sausage with the best of them. And head-cheese." She nodded her head. "Mor taught us how to season it just right." She looked at Nora for confirmation.

"And the hams." Nora joined her sister in the memory. "But where will we get the hickory for flavor?"

"Don't you worry." Carl patted his wife's shoulder as he rose to go back outside. "We know how to smoke the bacon here in North Dakota, too. You just get all the knives sharpened and the pans ready."

"Selling the meat will surely help buy feed for the winter." Nora cleared the table after he left. "Those grasshoppers ate nearly everything. Clara, I've never seen anything like it. So many they blotted out the sun. Only the root crops lived through it. Thank the good Lord the rains came and the grass grew again so the cows could pasture. And the hay was already in the barn."

Clara shuddered. Insects had never been her favorite friends. "Does that happen often?"

"I hope not."

Clara was still brushing her hair the next morning by

lamplight when she heard the dog barking and horse harnesses jingling. She could see her breath in the room, the night had turned so cold. As Carl had said, perfect butchering weather. A twinge of sorrow for the animals about to lose their lives crossed her mind. But at least here, she hadn't cared for them for months and played with the babies when they were tiny.

She braided her hair in back and coiled it in a bun at the nape of her neck. Wearing her worst dress covered with a huge apron, she felt ready for the day.

"You remember Dag Weinlander," Carl said when he brought the men in for coffee before beginning. "And this is Will, his helper." Carl introduced two other men. Clara nodded to each, secretly studying each face in case it matched her picture. She didn't bother to look too carefully at the blacksmith. It was obvious he hadn't washed since their first meeting. She wrinkled her nose and tended to pull away when she refilled his coffee cup.

"*Mange takk.*" Dag's deep voice surprised her.

"Yah." She responded automatically. The man could speak. She flinched inwardly. She could just hear her mother scolding her for thinking unkind thoughts about another of God's children. As she passed around the table with the coffeepot, she glanced up to catch him watching her. He ducked his head when he caught her eye.

The same thing happened at dinner. This time Clara could feel the heat rise on her neck. She shrugged off the feeling and headed back to the stove for another bowl of chicken and dumplings. She must be imagining things. But his voice stayed with her, even if the only exchange had been the polite "Thank you" and "You're welcome."

By the time she'd served the fresh fried liver for supper, Clara didn't care if she never saw a pig again. Or smelled the odors of blood and fresh meat. She and Nora had washed all the intestines to ready them for sausage casings and set both the shoulder and hindquarters to soak in brine before they could be smoked. They would have to grind the fat and begin rendering it out for lard the next day. And steam the krub, sausage made of round potatoes and the fresh blood. They'd serve that for dinner as a special treat.

"Come, little one," Clara lifted Kaaren onto her lap when she and Nora collapsed into the twin rocking chairs. Nora held the bottle for the nearly sleeping baby Peder. "You've been such a good girl today," Clara said as she snuggled the nightgown-clad child close.

"Pa made me a ball."

"Yah. That old pig bladder has a new use now." Clara looked to her sister, glad she didn't have to remind Nora of all the fun they'd had with pig bladders after butchering time. Her return smile said it all.

Kaaren leaned her head against Clara's shoulder. A yawn started with Kaaren and traveled from mouth to mouth to mouth. The little girl giggled as she yawned again. "Mr. Weinlander is a nice man."

Clara stopped rocking and stared down at the little one in her lap with eyes drooping shut. Where had that come from?

"He throwed my ball." The words spaced out as sleep overcame her.

What kind of a man is he, Clara thought as she snuggled down in the flannel sheets in her bed a few minutes later. She didn't have time to dwell on it or even say brief prayers before sleep closed her eyes like it had Kaaren's.

"Clara, I can't tell you how grateful I am for all your help," Nora murmured two nights later after they'd collapsed into the rockers again. The children were already in bed and the two sisters were enjoying a last cup of coffee and the quiet of a sleeping house.

"Yah, its been good." Clara lifted the cup to her lips and inhaled the rich aroma. "How come it was easier at home?"

"More of us and we had Mor to run things." Nora shrugged her shoulders up to her ears and rotated her neck from side to side. "And there were no little ones to help us the last few years."

"That is true." Clara pushed herself to her feet and went to open the oven door. She pulled a pan of browning ground lard forward and, with a large spoon, began skimming the melted fat off and pouring it into the bread pans. When she'd dipped all she could, she picked off a piece of the crispy remainder and popped it into her mouth. "We should make cornbread with some of these cracklings tomorrow."

"That sounds good." The yawn nearly cracked Nora's jaw. "Thank you, again." She pushed herself to her feet. "When all this is over, we'll have to start on English lessons for you." She patted a hand over the next yawn. "Good night. Sweet dreams."

Clara was too tired to even picture the curly haired man, let alone dream.

Nora had just pulled the pan of cornbread from the oven the next afternoon when they heard the dog barking.

Clara parted the starched white curtains to see out the window better. "It's Reverend Moen."

"And Ingeborge?"

"No, by himself."

Nora opened the door. "Come in, come in. You're just in time for hot cornbread and coffee."

"Thank you." He turned and shook hands with Carl who had come from the spring house. "And thank you for the side of pork." The two men shook hands. "We are truly grateful."

After the flurries of greetings, everyone gathered around the table. Clara cut the cornbread and, after placing the golden squares in bowls, drizzled maple syrup over the tops and passed the treat around the table.

By the time they'd poured the second cups of coffee,

most of the news had been shared. Reverend Moen cleared his throat. "While I appreciate the coffee and the visit, I really had a special purpose in coming out here today." He stopped and looked directly at Clara across the table. "We have an older woman in our congregation who is in need of help. . .Mrs. Gudrun Norgaard. Her husband died last winter and lately she hasn't been very well herself. She really needs someone to live with her all the time." He paused.

Clara could hear the kettle hissing on the stove.

"I thought of you, Clara. Would you be willing to move into town and help take care of Mrs. Norgaard?"

four

"Does she speak Norwegian?" Clara's voice squeaked on the last word.

Reverend Moen smiled and nodded. "Yes, and English and even some German. Her husband used to be the banker in town and, besides having an abundance of guests, they traveled."

"What will Clara be doing?" Nora asked. When she looked up from studying her coffee cup, the sheen of tears hovered in her eyes.

"She'll be companion, maid, and sometimes help the cook who is also the housekeeper. Mrs. Norgaard has spent much of her time in bed lately but the doctor feels someone young and lively will help her regain her strength." Reverend Moen smiled again at Clara. "I think our God provided the perfect person in you."

"But...but...." Clara clamped her lips together. *God, why?* she pleaded within her heart and mind. *This isn't what I thought You planned for me. I'm supposed to be getting married and...and,* she sent pleading looks to Nora, then Carl, and finally to Reverend Moen.

"How soon do you need to know her decision?" Nora

sat up straight in her chair.

"Mrs. Norgaard needs someone immediately since Mrs. Hanson, the cook, has to go home to care for her mother for a time. That was one reason I thought of Clara. I...we ...were hoping you could return to town with me. I'm sure Carl would bring in the remainder of your things when they come to church on Sunday."

"Yes, of course." Carl nodded as he spoke. "Nora, you would help her to get ready?"

Just a minute, Clara wanted to pound her fist on the table and make the dishes rattle. *You're deciding my life. I want to make my own decisions.* She bit off the thoughts before they could become full-blown words.

Reverend Moen leaned his elbows on the table and tented his fingertips. The silence in the room was broken only by the mewing of the cat at the door to go out.

Clara knew what an animal in the circus must feel like with everyone staring at it. She scrubbed the front of her teeth with the tip of her tongue.

"I don't want Auntie Clara to leave. I needs her here with me." Kaaren slipped from her mother's lap and ran around the table to cling to Clara's skirt.

Clara bent over and laid her cheek on the little girl's head. "I won't be very far away and I'm sure Mrs. Norgaard would love to have you come visit." Clara felt her stomach drop down around her knees. The decision was made. She'd just said so. She gave Kaaren an extra hug and, planting her hands on the table, pushed herself to her feet. "I'll be ready whenever you need me to be."

"It's not like you'll be across the ocean or some such," Nora reminded them both as she helped Clara gather her things and pack them in the well-worn carpetbag.

"I know." Clara removed her gray Sunday dress from the nail on the wall.

"And maybe by living in town, your young man will find you more easily."

And maybe not, Clara thought as she looked around the room for anything she'd forgotten.

"Just think, you'll be closer to Ingeborge. Why, you could run over to see her anytime you'd like."

Clara hefted the bag and marched out the door. Why did she feel like the red caboose being towed along by the steaming engine whether it wanted to or not? She shook her head at the thought. She had made the final decision— hadn't she?

After one more neck-wrenching hug from Kaaren, Clara allowed Reverend Moen to assist her into his buggy. She waved goodbye as he guided the horse in a circle to turn the buggy around and trot out the lane. When her heart wanted to send a plea heavenward, she stopped it. Right now she didn't want to talk with Him. Miffed was the word that came to mind. Could one be miffed at God? She resolutely closed her ears to the sound of her mother's admonishing voice.

Clara could feel Reverend Moen watching her in between guiding the trotting horse. She let herself relax against the back of the seat as he began whistling. When she recognized the tune, she sneaked a peak at the man beside her. Yes, the courage of *Onward Christian Soldiers* was what she needed right now.

"Why are you worried?" His voice was gentle, like the sun warming her shoulders.

"I. . .I've never cared for someone who is sick before. Or who lives in a grand house." She took in a deep breath and let it out in a sigh.

"You'll do just fine or I wouldn't have asked."

Clara fingered the corner of her picture through the fabric of her bag. Did she dare ask him if he'd remembered who the picture reminded him of? If he'd remembered, wouldn't he have told her? And anyway, if the man hadn't come forward by now, did she really want to know him?

Clara rubbed the spot between her eyebrows where frown lines showed. Her mother said lines like that showed one didn't trust God with everything. But it's hard to trust when things aren't going the way you thought they should. Clara continued listening to the arguing and questioning in her mind.

The raucous call of a crow from a willow by the creek caught her attention. He didn't sound too happy with his life right now, either. He flew off, black wings glistening in the sun.

Up ahead, Clara could see the outskirts of Soldall. The lonely whistle from the west-bound train floated back on the breeze. Smoke from the engine smudged the faded blue sky. Clara shivered as the late afternoon breeze warned them of the coming frost. Would she be lonely and cold like the crow and the train?

Reverend Moen turned his horse into the lane of a two-story square house surrounded by pillared porches. A leaf from one of the two sentinel elm trees floated down as he pulled the animal to a halt amid a rustling of leaves already hiding the ground.

Clara stared at the windows, all curtained or draped. The place was big, like a palace, and beautiful with it's white paint and dark shutters. But it certainly needed a bit of life, everything seemed so quiet.

"You ready?" Reverend Moen broke her concentration. "You know, if you really are unhappy here after trying it for a time, we'll find someone else."

Clara nodded. She took in a deep breath and let it out, while stretching her mouth into a smile. She clamped her teeth to stop the quiver in her chin. She squared her shoulders after Reverend Moen helped her alight. Maybe that way she'd feel more like one of those soldiers he'd been whistling about.

The woman who met them at the door must have been born smiling. "Come in, come in." She held open the dark oak door set with fancy cut glass. "I'm Mrs. Hanson and

I know you're Clara. Reverend Moen, she's all you said she would be. You just come right on in here and. . . ."

Clara felt like she'd been swamped by a wave of words and was being washed out to sea. At the same time, she caught her breath at the richness of the dark woods on the floor and walls, the carved stairs curving off to the left, and the fire crackling and snapping in the fireplace. A real fire, with wood, not the glow of coal.

"I thought a fire would make all of us feel better, so now you just sit down and make yourselves comfortable. Mrs. Norgaard, bless her heart, is taking a nap, she sleeps so poorly at night you know and she told me to make you feel right to home. Now I have the coffee almost ready and after Reverend Moen brings the rest of your things in, we'll just have a bite."

Clara nodded and did just what she was told. She didn't have to worry about what to say because the woman never took a breath. She felt a bubble of laughter rising like warm yeast down about her middle. All her worry and fears of the housekeeper's not liking her, all gone to waste.

And after she met Mrs. Norgaard, Clara's remaining fears took off like the crow they'd seen on the drive in. Even propped by pillows, the frail woman lay dwarfed by the carved, four-poster bed. A lace-trimmed cap covered yellowed gray hair and her eyes mirrored the sorrow she'd lived. The smile that nearly appeared flitted away before it could dimple the sunken cheeks.

"Thank you for coming so quickly."

Clara had to bend close to hear the words. "You are welcome. I hope that I can be of help to you."

"Mrs. Hanson has to leave in the morning so she'll show you where everything is."

Clara nodded.

Reverend Moen stepped up to the side of the bed. "I must be going now. I'll stop by tomorrow or Ingeborge will."

"Thank you." She sank back against her pillows as if the brief exchange had been too much.

Clara followed the reverend out the door. "Is she really so sick?"

"At heart. And when the heart is heavy, the body gets too tired to continue. She feels she has nothing left to live for and that she'd rather join her husband in heaven."

"But. . .but, how can I help her?"

"Ask our Heavenly Father, He'll tell you." Reverend Moen settled his hat back on his head. "Bless you." And with that he shut the door behind himself and went whistling down the walk.

The tune stayed in her mind. But who said she wanted to be a soldier anyway?

Clara trailed her fingers up the splendidly polished banister as she climbed the stairs. Her room was just across the hall from Mrs. Norgaard's and she paused at the door before turning back to check on her new charge. She tapped lightly and entered the dim room.

The first thing I'd like to do, she thought, is open those draperies and let the sun shine in. And get her sitting up in the chair in front of the window so she can watch the glorious leaves drifting down. Did they have squirrels in North Dakota? Surely they must.

"Is there anything I can get for you?" she asked gently.

"No, no thank you."

Clara waited by the bed. The silence matched the dimness of hue.

"You can go settle into your room. I'd like to sleep again."

Clara struggled with the faint order. She'd been hired to care for this poor sick woman. *God, what do You want me to do? How can I help her the best?* She waited, hoping against hope that God wouldn't mess this one up, like He had her marrying the young man in the picture.

Instead of God's voice, she heard her mother's. "A cheerful heart doeth good, like a medicine." Clara knew it was a quote from somewhere in the Scriptures, probably Proverbs. How was that supposed to help her?

"I will lift up mine eyes unto the hills, from whence cometh my help." Well, so much for that one, Psalm 121. The last hills she'd seen were just out of New York. Her mind's eye flitted to the mountains of Norway, the glistening peaks, and the granite faces. The wind singing through the pine trees. Now, those were hills worthy of lifting up one's eyes.

"Are you still here?" The faint voice was painted in querulous tones now.

"Yes, ma'am."

"What are you doing?"

"Praying, I think."

"Well, pray then that I may go home soon."

Clara thought of the hills and the strength they always gave her. "No, I think not." She turned around and strode to the tall windows, draped in a dusky rose velvet. With determined hands she pushed back the heavy lengths of fabric and then the sheer cream panels, tying both back with the cords at the sides. After checking the latches, she bent over and pulled up the sash.

"What are you doing? Young woman, ah. . . ."

"The name is Clara, Clara Johanson, and I'm letting in what little is left of today's sun and fresh air."

"I. . .I'll freeze. It's November, you know." The voice sounded stronger already.

"Now, why don't I help you over here so you can see out? And while you sit in the chair here, I'll straighten your bed and—"

"No, this is the height of foolishness. I'm ringing for Mrs. Hanson and she'll tell you what I can and cannot do." Mrs. Norgaard leaned over and pulled on a cord beside her bed.

"Good, then she'll help me help you." Clara closed the

window again and strode back to the bed. "Why don't we have her bring a tray with coffee and cookies on it at the same time. How do we go about telling her what we want?"

Mrs. Norgaard flopped back against her pillows, her hand pressed to her chest. "We want?" The words ended on a squeak.

"Mrs. Norgaard!" Mrs. Hanson stopped in the doorway. She stared from the windows to Clara and then to the woman in the bed. A smile started, immediately hidden by the clenching of her lips. Her eyes refused to match her mouth and instead, danced with delight.

"We'd like coffee and maybe something sweet, if you have it." Clara clamped her hands together. Was she understanding Mrs. Hanson right? "But if you could help me move Mrs. Norgaard to the chair first?" She nodded at the dainty upholstered chair by the low table. "We'll turn the chairs so we can watch the trees and the sunset." Clara suited her actions to her words.

"That sounds wonderful." Mrs. Hanson bent over the bed. "Up we go, my dear."

"But, but, I. . .I. . . ." Mrs. Norgaard found herself ensconced in the chair with a blanket over her knees and a shawl around her shoulders before she could so much as fluster.

"A tray will be right up." Mrs. Hanson left the room with a wink to Clara.

"I am so grateful you speak Norwegian," Clara said as she straightened the blanket and tucked it around Mrs. Norgaard's feet. "Now, is there anything I can get for you before I make up the bed?"

The little woman shook her head, her chin set at a pugnacious angle. The lace on her cap fluttered in the motion.

Lord, I sure hope I'm doing the right thing, Clara thought as she pulled off the covers and stripped off the sheets. Only the sounds of her actions rustled the silence of the room. The thought of Reverend Moen's whistling made her smile. What would happen if she began whistling? She knew how. Even though well-brought up young ladies did not whistle. She sighed. Whistling was out for now.

But the tune wasn't. Her mind fit the words with the melody, "Onward Christian Soldiers, marching as to war . . . ." Was this really a war going on here? She shook her head. No only a skirmish—and she knew who the winner would be.

"Where do you keep the clean sheets?"

"In the linen closet. You'll find it on your left in the hall." Mrs. Norgaard shifted in her chair. "Before you do that, could you please bring me that footstool? If it would be no trouble."

Clara did as asked and tucked in the blanket again. "I'll be quick."

"No hurry, I—ah, see the sun through the reds and golds of the tree leaves." She snapped her mouth shut as if afraid she'd said too much.

Clara put a clamp on her grin and hurried to finish her chore.

While the coffee time passed quickly, it wasn't because of the inspiring conversation. Mrs. Hanson joined them and, unlike her voluble self of the earlier hours, said very little. Her bright eyes missed nothing however, and her nod clearly expressed approval.

Mrs. Norgaard sipped her coffee and, after taking two bites of cake, crumbled the sliver of pound cake into her napkin. When she leaned her head against the back of her chair and let her eyes droop closed, Clara took pity on her.

"Here, ma'am, let's put you back to bed." She set the cup and saucer on the tray and clasped the older woman's delicate hands. Together, she and Mrs. Hanson helped Mrs. Norgaard back to bed.

She sighed as the covers were smoothed over her. "That did feel good. Thank you."

"I'll let you rest now, dinner won't be for another hour or so." Mrs. Hanson paused at the doorway. "Would you like yours up here on a tray, too, or would you come down?"

Clara shrugged in consternation. "What is best?"

"We have much to go over."

"Yah, that is right."

A deep sigh came from the vicinity of the bed.

The two women looked at each other, over at the bed, and then, covering their mouths with their hands, tip-toed out.

"Come down as soon as you've settled yourself in your room." Mrs. Hanson patted Clara's arm. "You'll do real well with her."

Clara opened the door to her room and immediately crossed to the windows to open the draperies. Why did everyone like it so dark in this house? She stood at the window, gazing at the long yard fronted by the street. Two young girls walked by, swinging empty lard pails that had contained their lunch. The sun was slipping downward as if in a hurry to get to bed.

Clara turned from the window and surveyed her new home. A canopied bed piled high with lace pillows and a crocheted spread took her breath away. Never had she slept in anything so grand. A lace-skirted dressing table with a triple mirror reflected the fading sunlight, and, on the opposite wall, a tall armoire stood open to receive her few clothes. Clara sank down on the edge of the bed. All this for her?

She traced the intricate pattern in the spread with one finger. The rose-colored coverlet underneath set the design off to perfection. She glanced up to catch her reflection in the mirror. Was that really Clara Johanson she saw and not some young woman born to all this wealth and beauty? She felt like pinching herself to make sure she wasn't dreaming.

"Speaking of dreaming, girl, you need to go downstairs and learn all you can before tomorrow when this house and that woman in there all become your responsibility." She spoke sternly but the girl in the mirror couldn't resist a wink.

By the time she returned to the haven of her room, she'd followed Mrs. Hanson through the entire house, learned where all the food was stored, how to stoke the cellar furnace with coal, the location of all the cleaning supplies, and tried to memorize a list of all Mrs. Norgaard's likes and dislikes. The recipe books were all in English, as were the books in the library. She needn't worry about the laundry or the deep cleaning because Mrs. Hanson expected to be back in a week or two at the most.

"Just keep doing what you started," Mrs. Hanson said as she puffed her way back up the stairs. "I've settled her for the night and she has a bell by her bed to call you with since the bell pull only rings downstairs. If you need anything fixed, we always ask Dag, the blacksmith, and anything else, Reverend Moen will help." She put a finger to her bottom lip. "I can't think of anything else—oh, the doctor is two streets over and one back. We have an account at Lars Mercantile for groceries and what else."

Clara felt like her head was spinning. What in the world had she gotten herself into—correction—what had she been gotten into?

"I'll be leaving right after breakfast so you get a good night's sleep now." Mrs. Hanson opened the door to Clara's room and, after lighting the lamp by the door, stepped back. "Good night, my dear, and God bless."

"And you." Clara staggered across the room and collapsed on her bed. No wonder people with grand big houses hired others to work for them. The thought of all the dusting to be done made her shudder. She hefted her carpetbag onto the bed and removed her few garments, hanging some in the armoire and laying others in the drawers. She placed her Bible on the stand by her bed next to the lamp and her brushes on the dressing table.

By the time she changed into a flannel nightgown and brushed her hair one hundred strokes, she could feel her eyelids drooping. She sank to her knees and leaned her elbows on the spread.

"Father in heaven," she paused, waiting for the right words to come. "Thank You for this day." She paused again. "I guess." She shook her head, her thumbs rubbing into her eyes. "Mor says to thank You for everything and while that doesn't seem to make much sense to me, I know Your word says that also. So thank You for Mrs. Norgaard and my new home and position in this beautiful house." She huffed out her breath. "And thank You that we haven't found my young man yet." She shook her head again. "Forgive me for not being very thankful. Amen." She started to rise and sank back down. "And please show me how to care for Mrs. Norgaard. How do I make her want to live again? Amen—again."

She blew out the lamp and climbed under the covers. Hands crossed on her chest, she stared at the canopy over her head. She thought back to the way she'd taken over in Mrs. Norgaard's room, ordering her around like that. Clara, I can't believe that was you, she told herself. Maybe God had a hand in it after all. She fell asleep with that thought in her mind.

A jangling snatched her back from the deep well of sleep.

five

Where was she? The jangling came again. Clara sat up in bed and threw back the covers. Mrs. Norgaard—the bell—was something wrong? She fumbled for the flint to light the candle then slid her feet into waiting slippers. Light in hand, she crossed the room and opened her door. The bell came again.

"Mrs. Norgaard, are you all right?" She knocked and opened the door almost in the same motion. Moonlight streamed in the windows, painting branch shadows on the floor.

"Please, I have to use the chamber pot. I'm afraid I might fall."

"Yes, of course." Clara set the candle and holder down on the table beside the bed, along with the weight of fear she'd shouldered with the bell jangle. Such a simple task and yet so important.

After she had Mrs. Norgaard tucked back in bed, Clara clasped the hand that lay on top of the coverlet. Gently she stroked the papery skin that stretched over bones so light as to be air-filled. "Is there anything else I can do for you?"

"You might sing again. You have a lovely voice—so

long since there's been any singing in this house." The words came slowly as if with great effort.

Clara closed her eyes and began to sing, "Beautiful Savior, King of creation, Song of God and Song of man...." When she finished the second verse, she picked up her candle and, leaving the door open a crack, made her way back to her own room. With both doors open, she would hear the summons more quickly.

This time when she crawled back into the bed, she, too, felt blessed by the music. She thought of all the years her Mor had sung her children to sleep just like this. Who'd have thought these songs of her childhood would play an important part in her life now?

By the time Mrs. Hanson left for her train in the morning, Clara was feeling like the train had run over her, or at least dragged her down the track. Mrs. Norgaard showed her restlessness by ringing her bell or pulling the cord every few minutes with something she either needed or wanted to tell Mrs. Hanson. The stairs were looking higher and higher with each trip.

"This is a good sign," Mrs. Hanson nodded up the stairs just before she left the house. "Herself is at least taking an interest in life again." She patted Clara's cheek. "I knew the minute I saw you, you'd be just what she needed. Now remember, I'll be back for the laundry and such. You spend as much time with Mrs. Norgaard as she allows." Her eyes twinkled. "Rather as much as you can talk her into."

Clara nodded. "I hope your mother will be well soon." She waved and then leaned her back against the door after closing it. "Because I wish you were back here already."

The bell tinkled from the second door on the right—upstairs.

"Coming." Clara checked her appearance in the long mirror over a carved walnut table in the hall. She smoothed one side back and reset the comb that held her wavy golden hair up and off her face. After fluffing the tendrils of hair that insisted on curling over her forehead and wrinkling her nose at the image in the mirror, she trotted up the stairs.

"Ma'am." Clara stepped to the side of the bed.

Mrs. Norgaard opened her eyes as if the effort were beyond her strength. "Is Mrs. Hanson on her way?"

"Yah and none too soon. It is a good thing we are not too far from the station."

"Could you help me sit up against my pillows?"

"I can do better than that." Clara crossed the room and picked up the oval-backed chair to bring it back by the bed. "Let's get you up in this while I freshen your bed. You must have a wrapper around here somewhere." She checked all the usual places—foot of the bed, coat tree, under the covers—and finally stepped to the carved walnut armoire and opened the doors.

The scent of lavender wafted out. Clara sniffed appreciatively and studied the garments hanging in front of her. Morning dresses, shirtwaists, bombazine skirts, all in rich fabrics and jewel colors. She reached out to stroke the sleeve of a sable fur jacket. Such luxury. Resisting the urge to lay her cheek against the sleek garment, she turned instead to the hooks on the door. Both shawl and wool robe hung there, plain hens among peacocks.

"Here, now." She carried the robe to the bed and smiled down at her charge. "Once you are sitting up, I could brush your hair for you. That was always a treat for me, when my older sister would brush my hair."

Mrs. Norgaard nodded and eased over to the side of the bed. Clara helped her sit upright and snuggled the robe around the thin shoulders. Once situated in the chair, the woman sat up straight, obeying the dictates of a lifetime.

Clara picked up the hairbrush from the dressing table and, after removing the cap and pins, began drawing it through the limp strands. She smiled when she heard a sigh of appreciation. "That does feel good, doesn't it?" She continued the long, even strokes. "Perhaps tomorrow I could wash it for you. Mrs. Hanson said you were about due for a bath. Think how wonderful soaking in the tub would feel." She leaned forward to peek around the woman's shoulder. Mrs. Norgaard's eyes were closed but a slight smile hovered at the corners of her mouth.

Clara felt like she'd just been given a gift. In for a penny, in for a pound, she thought, quoting one of her mother's often-used maxims. "I know you've had a great sorrow in your life. Tell me about your husband, Mr. Norgaard. What was he like? How did you meet?"

Clara waited. Maybe she should have kept her mouth shut? *God, please keep me from saying or doing the wrong things. I so want to help.*

"He was such a handsome young man, my Einer. I lived in Minneapolis with my parents and this young man came to work at the bank there. My father owned a store and he frequently sent me to the bank for him since I helped him with the accounts and behind the counter when he needed me."

Clara kept up the soothing motions. "So you met him at the bank?"

"No, I saw him at the bank. But we weren't introduced until church one Sunday." She chuckled softly. "Back then one didn't have the freedom of young folks now. We had to be properly introduced by an outside party. I think he bribed the pastor to introduce us." Only the risp of the brush and gentle breathing disturbed the silence.

"Such a smile he had." She shook her head. "And he was trying to be so proper, to impress my mother and father, you know. They stayed right on either side of me." She tipped her head back so Clara could reach the brow more easily. "Penny novels talked of love at first sight but I thought they were making that up—until Einer spoke to me." Silence fell again.

Clara peeked around to catch the sight of fat tears rolling down her charge's sunken cheeks. She fashioned the gray strands into a bun and pinned it high on the back of Mrs. Norgaard's head. Then, after placing the brush on the dressing table, she knelt in front of the older woman and covered the trembling thin hands with the warmth of her own.

The tears flowed unchecked. Mrs. Norgaard sat upright, as if her back touching the chair were a mortal sin. Her body remained perfectly still, except for the quivering hands and the coursing tears.

Clara felt like her heart was being torn from her chest. Tears burned at the back of her throat and behind her eyes. *Lord, God, have mercy on her. Bring healing for her grief.* She reached into her pocket for a clean handkerchief and gently wiped the tears away.

The clock on the tall dresser struck the hour, eleven chimes. Clara found herself counting them, as if at the end there might be some incident of great import. The last boing faded away.

"I believe I'd like to return to my bed, now." Mrs. Norgaard pushed herself upright using the arms of the chair, placed her hand on Clara's arm, and crossed to the bed. Once under the covers, she patted the sides of her hair. "Thank you, child. You were right, that did indeed feel good."

After Clara left the room she wasn't sure if Mrs.

Norgaard meant the hair brushing felt good, or maybe the talking—and the tears? She hummed the refrain of *Onward Christian Soldiers* all the way down the stairs and into the spotless kitchen. Soon, the whistling teakettle accompanied her.

"What we need in this house is some music," she told the pink geranium hanging in the kitchen window. A black-hatted chickadee landed on the tray attached outside the window where Mrs. Hanson left crumbs for the birds. "That's it." Clara spun in place. "A bird to sing. One of those golden canaries like my aunt had. I wonder where you would find one clear out here on the prairie?"

She thought about it as she sliced the bread to toast for dinner. Mrs. Hanson had made a pot of chicken soup before she left and now it was warming on the monstrous iron stove.

"I'll just have to ask Ingeborge when I can go see her. Nora said Ingeborge knows everything and everyone in Soldall." She cocked her head at the flower in the window. "I think you better learn to talk or, better yet, sing because if someone comes they will think I am surely losing my mind." The geranium wisely kept silent.

The peal of the doorbell brought Clara rushing downstairs again; she had just taken Mrs. Norgaard her dinner. By the time she reached the door, the thing clanged again.

"*Uff da,*" she muttered. "I'm coming." She reached to open the door. A man, face showing florid around a mustache more salt than pepper, all topped by a mashed down fedora, touted a black bag that gave away his identity without a word. "Doctor?"

"Yes, I'm Dr. Harmon." He took off his hat as he stepped across the threshold. "Mrs. Norgaard asleep?"

"No, I just took her dinner up to her." Clara moved back to give the portly man room to enter the hall. "May I take your coat?" She shut the door and, after helping him remove his black wool coat, hung it on the brass tree next to the hall table.

"Good, then I can talk with you first." He walked into the parlor like he'd been here many times before.

"Ah, would you like some coffee?" At his nod, she added, "And have you eaten. I could bring you some chicken soup."

"That sounds wonderful." Instead of sitting in the parlor, he followed her into the kitchen. "Why don't I join you in here. Make it easier for all." Just then the bell pull sounded. "Ah, herself is callin' you. She wants to know who's here, no doubt. You run up and I'll just pour myself a cup of coffee and make myself to home." He suited his actions to his words and pulled out a chair at the round oak table in the corner.

Clara darted a look over her shoulder to make sure he was all right and climbed the stairs. She made a point of not counting how many times she'd been up and down them already today.

"You've hardly touched your soup," Clara said before her patient could respond. "And here it was nice and hot. Mayhap I should bring you another bowl."

Mrs. Norgaard shook her head. "No, I had a bit. Now, who is it that came? I thought I heard Dr. Harmon's voice."

"That's right. He's going to eat downstairs first, then he'll be up. Or. . . ," eyes narrowed, Clara studied her patient, "or, he can eat up here with you." She spun out the door. "I'll be right back." She descended the stairs in a swirl of skirts and indecision. Should she take charge here or not? Would the company make Mrs. Norgaard eat better, maybe smile? Let's see, they could move that table from over by the window and put it up against the bed. Then chairs for her and the doctor.

She smacked one fist into the palm of the other hand. She would turn this into a party yet.

Doc Harmon beamed at her, all the while nodding his head while she shared her plan. Together they set two trays with soup in a rose-sprigged tureen, coffee in a silver server, and buttered toast nestled by a pot of jam. Clara included a plate of sour cream sugar cookies for dessert. Like two conspirators in a crime, they set out.

"Good day, Mrs. Norgaard. We've come to share our dinner with you." He set his tray on the dressing table and crossed the room to bring the round table to the bed. "Now, would you rather have a chair or dangle your feet over the edge of the bed. Clara says you've already been up for a while this morning."

Mrs. Norgaard could hardly get a squeak in edgewise.

Just as they had the furniture all rearranged and Mrs. Norgaard moved to her chair, the doorbell pealed again. Clara dashed down the stairs and pulled up at the door, feeling like she was flying apart.

"Reverend Moen." She stepped back and motioned him inside.

"Good day, Clara. How is Mrs. Norgaard today."

"Would you like to come up and join us for coffee? Or soup? Dr. Harmon and I were just about to eat."

"Coffee yah, soup, *nei takk*," he said as he hung up his coat.

"You go on up, I'll get another cup." Clara dashed off to the kitchen. Talk about having a party.

When she got upstairs, Dr. Harmon had settled his patient in her chair, pulled up two more, and dished up the soup. Clara finished pouring the coffee and asked Reverend Moen to say grace. As the familiar words flowed forth, Clara could feel herself back home in Norway, with her family gathered around the dinner table.

At the "Amen", she looked up to see Mrs. Norgaard reach up with a tentative hand to smooth her already sleek hair.

I'm glad I did her hair this morning, Clara thought. No woman likes to have company when she feels a sight.

It was quickly obvious that the two men were good friends who liked to give each other a bad time. And as Clara suspected, her patient forgot her lack of hunger and downed both soup and toast.

By the end of the meal, Clara knew all the latest news of Soldall. A young boy had fallen out of a tree at recess over at the school and sprained his wrist. His mother threatened to break his arm if he didn't stay out of trees. Doc had agreed with her.

"That young whippersnapper is an accident waiting to happen, not waiting as the case may be." The doctor snorted after telling his story. "He can get into more mischief."

"Isn't he the one who put a mouse in the new teacher's desk drawer?" Reverend Moen asked.

The doctor nodded. "And the frog in the water pail."

Clara squeezed her lips together. It sounded like they were describing her younger brother. Mor had been afraid Lars wouldn't make it to manhood.

"Well, I must be on my way," Doctor Harmon finally said after pulling out his pocket watch and checking the time. "This has been most enjoyable, Mrs. Norgaard. Thank you for your hospitality. How about if I check you over before I leave?"

"And I, too, must be going. Good day, Mrs. Norgaard." Reverend Moen patted her hand. "This has been a real pleasure."

"Thank you for coming." Mrs. Norgaard let the men assist her to her feet and back to the edge of the bed. "Perhaps next time you come, you could bring your daughter, Mary."

"I'll do that. Clara, here, let me help you take these things downstairs." He picked up the larger of the trays and waited while Clara added the bowls and cups to it. Together, they took the trays back to the kitchen.

"Do you need anything?" the reverend asked as he placed his tray on the kitchen table.

Clara shook her head. "No, wait, I mean yes. Do you know anyone who has a canary?"

"A canary?"

"Yes, for sale." Clara set her tray down. "You see, it is so quiet here, not a sound, so I thought the bird would sing and make Mrs. Norgaard feel happier."

"How about a kitten instead? They're easier to find."

"But they don't sing too well."

"True." Reverend Moen rubbed the bridge of his nose in the gesture that Clara already knew meant he was thinking. "I'll ask Ingeborge." He walked down the front stairs still chuckling about her wanting a yellow bird to sing.

"I think that's a good idea," Doctor Harmon said when Clara asked him about the canary. "Might be just what the doctor ordered—if he'd thought of it." He shrugged into the coat Clara held for him. "Now don't you worry so much about the house and spend your time with her. I'll see you again in a day or so."

Clara leaned against the door after they'd left. She could feel the silence settling back down on the house. The bell tinkled from upstairs.

The next morning she talked Mrs. Norgaard into a bath and hair washing. Each time she asked about Mr. Norgaard and each time Mrs. Norgaard shared a bit more. And each time the tears flowed.

One night after she'd helped Mrs. Norgaard to bed, Clara sat on the edge of the mattress to say good night.

"Don't go." The old woman clutched the hand of the younger. The silence settled around them, close and comforting this time, as if in benediction.

"This is the hardest time," Mrs. Norgaard spoke from the dimness. "When the lights are out and all my memories crowd in, piling on top of each other, pushing and shoving until I can't sleep, can't rest." The silence reigned again. "And when I feel so guilty."

"Guilty?"

"Yes, I should have been able to help him more. If only I'd made him stay home and go to bed when he first felt ill." Clara waited. "And if I'd thrown out those awful, smelly cigars maybe he wouldn't have had a cough to start with." Her voice floated on the stillness, like a leaf kissing the surface of a pond.

Clara stroked the papery hand that lay in hers. *Father,* she prayed while she waited for the voice to come again, *please bring healing to Mrs. Norgaard. Help her to give up the bad feelings. Help her to want to live.* The thoughts seemed to drift heavenward, like smoke rising from a chimney on a still, winter day.

"Einer insisted on going out to that farm with Dr. Harmon. So many people were sick that the well ones did what they could, chores and such. I was helping Mrs. Moen. She collected extra children and housed them until their parents could care for them again. Ah, me. Maybe I was the one who brought the sickness home." Silence again. "We'll never know."

Clara could hear the tears begin to drown out the woman's voice.

"But he was so sick. I was right here beside him. He'd been tossing and turning and finally settled down. I. . .I thought he was finally resting so I dozed off myself. When I woke up. . . ."

Clara squeezed her eyes closed but the tears refused to be swallowed.

"When I woke. . .he was gone." Deep sobs, the kind that come after being forced back too long, shuddered through her frame, shaking the bed.

Clara gathered the straining body into her arms and held her. What could she say, even if she could talk around the tears that rained down her own cheeks?

Mrs. Norgaard reached for the edge of the sheet to wipe her eyes. "I never...," she choked on the words, "I never said goodbye. He was gone and I never said goodbye. Did he know how much I loved him?"

Sobs interrupted her words, making them difficult to understand but Clara murmured soothing noises, whispering the litany of love she'd learned at her mother's knee.

Eventually, hiccups punctuated the silence and Clara placed a handkerchief in Mrs. Norgaard's hand. After blowing her nose, the now-spent woman lay back on her pillows. She put her hand back in Clara's. "I'm sorry to get you so wet."

"I'll dry."

"Do you think God will forgive me?"

"For what?"

"For being so angry at Him for taking my Einer." She paused. "For wanting to die."

"All you have to do is ask. Mor says He forgives even before we ask, that's what sending His Son to die for us meant. Forgiveness and love that never dies."

"Your mother is a wise woman." Mrs. Norgaard blew her nose again. Her sigh snagged on a leftover sob.

Clara could feel the yawn that caught Mrs. Norgaard and then sneaked up on Clara. She covered her mouth with her hand but still felt the hinges in her jaw creak with the strain.

"Thank you, my dear." Mrs. Norgaard breathed deeply and patted Clara's hand. "You go on to bed now, I'll be just fine." She yawned again. "In fact, I'm almost asleep already."

"I can sit here for a while. There's no hurry."

Clara was about to rise from the bed, thinking her charge almost asleep, when Mrs. Norgaard said with a catch in her voice.

"Would you. . .do you know the Twenty-third Psalm?"

"Yah, I do. We memorized that in Sunday School when we were small."

"Would you say it for me?"

Clara closed her eyes and thought of the shepherd with his flock. "The Lord is my shepherd, I shall not want. He maketh me to lie down in green pastures, he leadeth me beside the still waters. . . ." Her voice caught in the part about the valley but grew stronger again as she came to "And I will dwell in the house of the Lord forever."

"Amen."

"Yah, Amen." Clara nodded. When she rose a few minutes later, Mrs. Norgaard was breathing the soft and even rhythm of healing sleep.

"Thank You, thank You, thank You." Gratitude poured forth as Clara blew out the lamps and undressed for bed. Even while her mind sang the praises, her body felt like a garment with all the starch washed out. She was asleep almost before her head touched the pillow.

When Clara walked into Mrs. Norgaard's room with the coffee tray in the morning, Mrs. Norgaard was sitting up against her pillows.

"I want you to go over to Reverend Moen's this morning and ask him to come here." Even her voice was stronger.

"Tell him I'm ready now."

Whatever for, Clara wondered, but she only nodded, a smile tickling the corners of her mouth.

six

She had a feeling this was more like the real Mrs. Norgaard.

The doorbell rang before Clara could finish her duties and get out the door. She answered the chimes, still wiping her hands on her apron.

"Good morning, Clara." Doc Harmon tipped his hat with one hand, the other carrying his black leather bag. "How is our patient this morning?"

"Better, I think." Clara stepped back and motioned him in. "She wants me to go for Reverend Moen."

"Whatever for?" Doc laid his hat on the hall table and brushed a hand over his steel gray hair.

Clara shrugged. "Maybe if you ask her, she'll tell you."

"And maybe she won't. The won't is much more likely." Doc started up the stairs. "Do you by any chance have the coffee hot? I've been out delivering a baby north of town and I could use a pick-me-up."

"Yah, I do. There's bread and some cheese if you'd like." She waited with her hand on the carved ball of the walnut newel post.

"Fine. And after you've brought it up, you can run over to the reverend's. I'll stay and visit that few minutes."

Clara did as asked and, within a few minutes, darted out

86

the front door. It was the first time she'd been out since Reverend Moen brought her here. She drew in a deep breath of air redolent of burning leaves and crisp fall weather. As she kicked her way through the leaves blanketing the ground she looked up through the naked tree branches stretching to the lemony sun in the watery blue sky. If the weather patterns were the same here as in Norway, it felt like a storm hovering on the horizon.

She turned to the left and walked briskly down the packed dirt street. She passed the houses, playing the I wonder who lives there game that she and Nora used to play on their way to school. But in Norway it was I wonder what they're doing there, since they knew all the inhabitants of their small village.

It was different here. Clara refused to allow the worm of homesickness dig it's way into her beautiful day. She thought back to the night before instead. "The Lord is my shepherd...," she sang the song, the ancient words set to a tune they'd learned in Sunday School. Why was it she always felt better when she began singing? How much easier it was to remember Bible verses when they'd been set to music.

She sang her way up a cross street and down the main street until she saw the white picket fence of the Moen home. When she knocked on the door, the reverend himself answered it, his shirt sleeves rolled up to his elbows.

"Clara, how wonderful to see you. Come in, come in." He stepped back, opening the door wide in welcome.

"What brings you to our house? Ingeborge, we've company."

Clara stopped inside the door. "I can't stay but a minute. Doctor Harmon is with Mrs. Norgaard so I could do what she asked."

"And what is that?"

"She said for you to come now, she was. . .is ready." Clara recited the words, hoping the man in front of her would understand the meaning.

"That's all?" He rubbed the bridge of his nose with one finger, his right hand tucked under his left elbow.

Clara nodded.

"Oh, I'm so glad you are here. Sit down, sit down. John, you haven't taken her coat yet. What is this world coming to?" Ingeborge whirled down the last of the stairs and enveloped Clara in a hug that left no doubt as to her joy. She leaned back and studied the younger woman's face. "You look like caring for Mrs. Norgaard is agreeing with you."

"Yah, it is. Such a beautiful place." Clara patted Grace on the head and squatted down to say hello to little James. "But I must get back."

"The coffee will be ready in a minute."

"Another time, *mange takk*. Reverend, you will be coming?"

Ingeborge looked from one to the other, her eyes bright and dimples ready to leap into view with the least encouragement. "Is Mrs. Norgaard feeling up to visitors?"

"She asked for Reverend Moen."

"She isn't worse, is she?" The dimples dove into hiding.
"*Nei, nei.* I think she's better."

Reverend Moen rolled down his sleeves preparatory to
putting on his coat even as they talked. "I shouldn't be
long." He removed his hat from the hall stand and, putting
it on, went out the door, only to return. "Would you rather
stay a few minutes to visit or walk with me?"

"Oh, stay," Ingeborge pleaded.

Clara felt like a length of cloth being pulled at both ends.
Duty won over and she smiled her apology. "Another
time. Perhaps you and the children could come to call
soon. That house is so silent. It needs the sound of children
laughing."

"We will." Ingeborge patted Clara's arm. "I'm happy
that you like it there. I'm sure Mrs. Hanson is grateful she
needn't worry about her charge."

"*Farvel,*" Clara said as she waved goodbye from the
steps. She trotted after Reverend Moen who waited for her
at the gate. Halfway down the walk, Clara spun around and
darted back to the porch. "Do you know anyone who might
have a canary for sale? I think the bird's song would cheer
Mrs. Norgaard up. And it would make some music in that
still house."

Ingeborge shook her head, her brow wrinkling in thought.
"Not now, but I'll ask around. That's a wonderful idea.
Farvel." She stood in the doorway, waving until they were
up the street.

Reverend Moen set a brisk pace and Clara found herself
trotting to keep up with his long strides. When they arrived

back at the Norgaard place, they met Doctor Harmon just coming down the stairs.

"I don't know what you've done, my dear, but keep it up, whatever it is." He shrugged into his coat and picked up his hat. "I'll check back in a couple of days. Now Reverend, don't go messing with my patient."

Clara could tell he was teasing by the twinkle in his eye.

"She's on the mend so you can't have her yet."

"And I'm sure you think your medicine did the trick?" Reverend Moen tried to look serious and failed utterly.

"What else?" The doctor chuckled as he strode out the door, waving one hand behind him.

"You go on up," Clara took the reverend's coat at the same time she heard the summoning bell from upstairs. "I'll warm up the coffee."

By the time Clara had the tray ready, she met Reverend Moen trotting back down the stairs.

"I'll be right back." He grabbed his coat and slipped out the door, hitting the ground running. He turned and jogged backwards. "Don't worry," he called back. "It's good news."

Clara shook her head as she climbed the stairs. What a strange day this was turning out to be.

"Just put the tray over there." Mrs. Norgaard pointed to the table in front of the windows. "We'll wait for Reverend Moen and serve then. Do you think you could brush my hair before he gets back?"

Clara set the tray down and turned to find Mrs. Norgaard sitting on the edge of her bed, slipping her arms into the sleeves of her robe. Clara paused to see what her patient would do next. Mrs. Norgaard belted and tied the sash then looked up.

"Could you please help me to the chair? I know it's easier for you when I'm there." She took Clara's arm and raised herself to her feet. Clara waited while Mrs. Norgaard swayed a bit and then steadied herself. "I'm weak as a kitten." The tone was colored in exasperation.

Clara felt like singing as she brushed the long, gray tresses. What could have brought on the change? Their talk last night? The tears? Her prayers? Probably a combination of all three but whatever—Clara gave God all the glory. Her whispers of "Thank You, thank You" played counterpoint to the melody.

When Reverend Moen returned a few minutes later, he carried a small leather case along with his Bible. Reverently he removed an embroidered stole and placed it around his neck. Then he set out his communion supplies.

So that's what she was ready for. Clara tucked the last pin in the coil of hair on the back of Mrs. Norgaard's head.

"I'd like the chairs over by the window, if you please." Mrs. Norgaard looked up at Clara. "Thank you, my dear. That felt wonderful. I believe you have the gift of healing in those hands of yours."

Clara held her hands out in front of her, turning them over and back. Could that be? They looked just like her hands had all her life. No different. She shook her head.

"Here, let me help you while Reverend Moen moves the chairs." After seating Mrs. Norgaard, Clara turned to leave the room.

"No, please stay. I'll feel more like we're in church if it isn't just me." Mrs. Norgaard clutched Clara's hand.

Clara nodded.

But I'm not prepared, she thought. I haven't time to review my sins. When was the last time I received communion? So long ago. Clara took one of the chairs and folded her hands in her lap. She breathed deeply, letting all the air out till her shoulders slumped. She closed her eyes.

Reverend Moen began reading. "From Chapter One of First John. 'That which was from the beginning. . .God is light and in him is no darkness. . .But if we walk in the light as he is in the light. . .If we say we have no sin, we deceive ourselves. . .If we confess our sin, he is faithful and just to forgive us our sins and to cleanse us from all unrighteousness.' Let us be quiet now and confess those sins that stand between us and Him."

Clara thought back over the last weeks. *I confess that I doubted You,* she thought. *I know I have not always come to You first but tried to do things on my own. I doubted that You have a plan for my life and I resented not meeting the man in my picture.* She continued thinking about the things she had done wrong. *Father, forgive me,* she prayed. *I don't want anything to stand between us.*

Reverend Moen flipped to Matthew, Chapter Twenty-six in his Bible and began again, this time with the last supper.

At Jesus' words, Clara could feel the tears clogging the

back of her throat. 'This is my body. . .this is my blood of the new testament, which is shed for many for the remission of sins.' When she had finished the communion she wiped the flowing tears away with the corner of her apron.

Mrs. Norgaard reached over and borrowed the other corner. She sniffed and wiped her tears again with the backs of her fingers. The sigh seemed to come from the depths of a soul released from bondage and now ready to walk in the fullness of God's light and freedom.

"Now remember those words, He not only forgives but cleanses us." Reverend Moen closed his Bible and made the sign of the cross. "The Lord bless you and keep you. The Lord lift up His countenance upon you and give you His peace. Amen."

"Amen." The two women chimed together.

A chorus of angel choirs could not have been richer than the quiet that filled the room and made its home in her heart. Clara recognized peace when she felt it.

Time passed but no one disturbed it until Mrs. Norgaard sighed deeply and raised her head. "Thank you, Reverend Moen. I believe I can go on now. I know that Einer is with our Father and I will be, too, one day, but I guess that day hasn't come yet. Not for me anyway."

She reached over and took Clara's hand. "So we'll just have to get me well again. Right?"

Clara nodded. She covered Mrs. Norgaard's hand with her own. "God willing."

"Oh, I think *He's* been willing all along. It's this stubborn old woman who wanted to go the other way."

After Clara rewarmed the coffee and served, she settled Mrs. Norgaard down for a nap and walked Reverend Moen to the door. "Thank you for a beautiful service."

"All I did was read God's Word. We forget how wonderful and powerful it is, especially when read aloud. As told in Matthew, Chapter Eighteen, He meant it when He said 'For where two or three are gathered in my name, there am I in the midst of them.' "

Clara leaned her cheek against the edge of the open door. "I felt it. . .His presence. . .I mean. I feel like laughing and crying, both at the same time." She wiped away a tear with her finger tip. "Thank you so much."

"You're most welcome. I felt and feel the same. These moments make all my days worthwhile." He placed his brown felt hat squarely on his head. "God bless."

Clara felt the "God bless" for the rest of the day and through the evening. She felt it when she gave Mrs. Norgaard a back rub.

"Tell me how you came to this country," Mrs. Norgaard asked when she was settled against her pillows again.

Clara leaned back against the chair. As she related the story of the stained letter and the picture of the curly haired man, she could feel a difference. She didn't resent God for "messing things up" as she'd thought before.

"I had to confess being angry today because I thought God wasn't playing fair. I thought I understood He was bringing me to America to be a wife—right away. Even though I didn't know the man, I thought God would make it all right."

"And He didn't?"

"I don't know. No one seems to recognize the picture. No one has come forward to say 'Where's my wife, the one I bought a ticket for and who never showed up.'" Clara leaned her head back against the frame. "But after today, it isn't so important."

"Well, I shall always be grateful He brought you here, however He did it." Mrs. Norgaard folded her hands across her chest. "I know most of the people around here. Why don't you bring the picture here and show it to me?"

Clara thought about the suggestion. "Would you mind if we waited until morning when the light is better?"

"That would be fine." The quiet settled back. "Would you recite the Twenty-third Psalm again. That is such a comfort."

The words fell into the quiet of the room and the peace of their hearts, spreading like ripples on a pond.

When Clara fell into bed, she could only whisper, "Thank You, *mange takk*."

She woke to a day filled with the brightness of sun glinting off frost. It glittered on the trees and the frost fronds painted on the edges of the windows.

After breakfast she took her picture in to Mrs. Norgaard. Clara studied the older woman's face as she studied the picture. Clara saw the jaw clench and the cords stand out in Mrs. Norgaard's birdlike neck.

"Clara, please go over to the blacksmith's and bring Dag

back with you. I want to talk with him."

"Now?"

"Now!"

seven

Whatever could she want Dag for?

Mrs. Norgaard peered at Clara over the spectacles perched on her nose. "Well?"

"Yes, ma'am." Clara turned and hustled out of the room. She stripped off her apron and hung it on the hook at the same time reaching for her gray wool shawl. While her hands went about their chores, her mind worried at the question like a dog with a bone. What would Dag have to do with her picture? She thought again of the taciturn blacksmith. Hopefully he talked to others more than he did her.

She flew down the stairs and out the door, catching her breath at the bite of the breeze. Her nose tingled and began to run as quickly as her feet. While the sun was gorgeous, winter not only nipped her nose but bayed hard on the heels of fall.

Clara paused a moment at the wrought iron gate and raised her face to the sun. Eyes closed, she savored the hint of warmth and freshness of the world outside the silent house. She would have to get outside more, that's all there was to it.

She felt like skipping down the street and, after checking to see no one was watching her, did just that. Back in Norway, she might have been racing Lars over the hills or riding their fjord pony up to the summer hut where they took the cows to pasture in the warm season. Thoughts of home killed all desires for skipping.

What would Mor and Far be doing now? She scrunched up her eyes to think better. What part of the day was it in Norway now? She shook her head, letting the shawl fall back on her shoulders. Home was so far away, like another life. She rolled her lips together and looked up to the sky above. Her prayer winged upward like the steam rising from the roof tops. *Keep them safe,* she prayed, *and let us be together sometime again. Mange takk for this wonderful day and the new friends I am making.*

The picture of Else, her best friend since beginning school, took over her mind. But Else was already married and expecting her first baby.

Clara sighed and turned the corner to the blacksmith's shop. She'd just have to make a new best friend along with the new life in this new country. She glanced up the street to the fields beyond. This new, extremely flat, and amazingly huge country.

She had her smile back in place when she stopped in front of the weathered building, open to the street, with BLACKSMITH in black iron letters across the face. She wrinkled her nose at the distinctive aroma of trimmed horse hoof. A gray horse stood on three legs, it's rear forth clamped between Dag's knees.

"Hello, *frøken* Johanson," called Will from his place holding the horse's head.

"Hello, Will." Clara smiled at the lanky lad and waited, expecting Dag to join in the greeting.

The man bending over the shoe, tapped home another nail, set down his hammer, and picked up the crimper.

Clara waited.

"Fine day, isn't it?" Will shifted to the near side of the

horse.

"Yah, that it is." Clara looked back to Dag. He finished crimping the nails over, set aside the crimper, and picked up the rasp.

"Can we do something for you?" Will looked from Dag to Clara. He caught her gaze, glanced back at the man bending over the hoof and shrugged.

Clara felt a little fume begin about her heart region and make it's way to her mouth. She clicked her tongue against her teeth. *Had the man no manners at all? After all, it wasn't as if they were strangers.*

Dag eyed the final balance of the hoof and straightened. With a gloved hand he stroked the horse's haunch and made his way around to the other side.

He could feel a burn rising from his chest and up his neck. *What could she possibly want? Was this a social call? Who made social calls to the blacksmith? Mercy, but she was beautiful. The sun setting her hair afire, above eyes the green of a newly risen field of wheat.* He clamped a lid on his thoughts with the same strength he pounded iron.

He also forbade himself to peek around the horse's rear to see if she were still there. Why couldn't he just say "Hello" like Will did? Such an easy thing—for most people. If he dusted off his shirt and walked over to her, would she smile at him, like she had the boy?

The horse snorted, breaking a silence that stretched like a spider web between two blades of grass.

Clara cleared her throat. Why this urge to yell at him?

Dag rubbed his chin with the back of his pigskin gloves. Just a simple "Hello."

"Tell your master that Mrs. Norgaard would like to see

him, if he can find the time." *Or the words,* she wanted to add but nearly drew blood biting her tongue.

"Yes ma'am." Will ducked his head.

Clara spun around, her skirts swirling about her legs. Her steps jarred her knees. Insufferable—rude—crude. Each word matched each stomp.

"Tell Mrs. Norgaard I'll be there as soon as I finish shoeing this horse." The deep voice echoed up the dirt street after her.

Clara straightened her spine and her shawl. "Tell her yourself." Her mutter carried no farther than her shoulder.

Even though she'd smiled at a woman on her way to the store and nodded at a man in a wagon who raised his hat in greeting, Clara smacked her hand against the latch on the gate. The gate flew open, clanging against the fence. The sound jerked her back from casting dire consequences upon the head of the man who couldn't be bothered to be civil.

She carefully closed the gate behind her and switched her stomping to a normal gait while at the same time forcing herself to search the two naked elm trees for squirrels. A crow chastised her from the peak of the second-story dormer.

Clara inhaled a deep breath of the sparkly air, mounted the steps, and, by the time she entered the house, had herself totally under control. After trotting up the stairs, she hung up her shawl, retied her apron, and peeked in on Mrs. Norgaard.

The bed stood empty. Clara opened the door all the way and discovered her employer sitting in a rocker in front of the window. Clara swallowed her amazement.

"Could you please fix my hair before he comes?"

Clara nodded and picked up the brush and pins from the dressing table. As she brushed the long hair, she tried to think of something to say. Should she tell Mrs. Norgaard that Dag had been, well, less than helpful? But then he had said he'd come. She heaved a sigh and continued her ministrations.

"Wouldn't you rather tell me about it?" Mrs. Norgaard leaned into the rhythmic strokes of the brush.

"About what?"

"Whatever upset you. I watched you come through the gate—and up the walk."

"Oh." Clara tucked several hairpins in her mouth—to keep from answering or to be more efficient? She braided the long strands, looped the braid into a figure eight and inserted the pins. That left her with an empty mouth and, after thinking about her trip to the blacksmith's, with an empty smile.

"I—" The bell pealed from the front door.

"Show him up and bring us a coffee tray in about fifteen minutes." Mrs. Norgaard patted Clara's arm. "We'll talk later."

On the way down the stairs Clara considered. Had that last comment been a threat or a promise? Either way— why did that man have to be so infuriating? Her heels clicked on the stairs, each step reminding her that now it was her place to be polite—or not.

She opened the door, her normal welcoming smile tucked safely away.

Dag stood there, porkpie hat clutched between his hands.

Clara motioned him in and led the way up the stairs. She could feel his eyes burning holes into her back. She held herself rigidly straight, her chin at an angle that brooked no appeal. Only the slight trembling of her fingers as they trailed up the banister revealed the effort it took. If he could be silent, so could she.

Dag knew the way. He'd been to the house often, repairing the stove and installing the pump and piped-in water. The iron fence surrounding the property had been hand-formed in his own shop. He sniffed appreciatively. A fragrance of lavender drifted back from the starchy figure ascending the stairs before him. The rustle of her skirts made him conscious of the trim anatomy, rounded where it should be and slender, especially in the ankles.

He jerked his attention to the hand trailing the banister. That, too, slender, with long fingers, dainty but very capable. How gentle those hands had been with the children on the Detschman farm.

Enough! He focused his gaze on his boots. Dusty, bits of mud and probably—oh, if only he could go outside, clean them off, and start all over again. If only he could fly back to the smithy and answer the blond angel that had said "Hello" in a way that set his heart to hammering. Hammering louder than the sledge upon steel to sharpen a plowshare.

She pushed open the door and motioned him through. "Mr. Weinlander." He heard the sheet of ice tinkle and crackle around him as he walked through.

"Good morning, Dag." Mrs. Norgaard called from her window seat. "Please, come sit with me while Clara brings us some coffee. And make sure you bring three cups, my dear."

Dag sat, dwarfing the chair with his broad shoulders and tall body. He glanced back in time to see Clara glare daggers at him one more time before she turned and, after closing the door with a definite snap, tap away down the hall. If she'd called him a vile name, he wouldn't have felt it more.

He sighed and turned his attention to his hostess who gave away her awareness of his turmoil by a gentle smile.

Her words however were, as always, politely correct. After asking about his health, the weather, and the state of the smithy, Mrs. Norgaard leaned forward and picked up a picture from the table. "Please look at this and tell me who you think it is?" She handed the stained and faded likeness to him.

Dag studied the curly haired man in the photograph. He looked up, puzzlement wrinkling a brow barely peeping from behind the wild hair. "It is Jude, my brother, as you well know."

Mrs. Norgaard nodded. "Yes, I thought as much."

"But where...?" Dag studied the picture again. "Where did you get this?"

"That I'll tell you another time. But for now. . .where is he?"

Dag shook his head, the matted and twisted hair swinging in the force of it. "I don't know. He stopped one day . . . ," Dag wrinkled his brow remembering, "to tell me to take care of Ma. He was going to be gone for a while."

Silence but for the ticking clock filled the room. Mrs. Norgaard waited.

Dag nodded. "He told me to pick up a woman, *frøken* Johanson, at the station and take her to the Detschman farm. That is all."

"And you haven't seen him since?"

Dag shook his head again. "Is something wrong?"

Mrs. Norgaard reached for the picture and laid it face down on the table. "No, I think not." She clasped her hands loosely in her lap. The silence returned. "Did he marry that woman over in Hammerston?"

Dag started. Did she know *everything* that went on? "Maybe that's where he went but he'd have invited Ma to the wedding at least—I think." He twisted the hat in his hands. What was going on here?

Mrs. Norgaard sighed and nodded at the same time, as if she'd come to a decision.

Dag waited, expecting her to either continue the discussion or tell him what to do next. He'd learned long ago that one didn't rush Mrs. Norgaard and that no one in town or the surrounding counties, treated him with more care and civility.

Clara entered the room, carrying a tray laden with coffeepot, cups, and a plate of apple cake.

Dag nearly tipped the armless, needlepoint chair as he leaped to his feet to take the tray from her. She relinquished the ebony handles, losing her hands in his for just a moment. She resisted the urge to dust them off on her apron. Funny, a tingle like a spark had gone up her arms. She moved the picture of her man off the table so Dag could set the tray down. What was her picture doing here? Had Mrs. Norgaard shown it to Dag?

Her thoughts chased each other like squirrels in an oak tree. All the while, her hands poured the coffee, passed it and the cake around with the napkins, and took her own chair. She glanced up in time to see a look of pleasure cross Dag's face as he chewed and swallowed her cake, then sipped the coffee from a cup nearly hidden in his hand.

"More, Mr. Weinlander?" She offered the cake plate again. And again. Until there were only crumbs. Goodness, had the man never had apple cake?

When the coffeepot, too, was empty, Dag set his plate and cup on the tray and, picking up his hat again, stood to go. *"Mange takk."* He nodded both to the old woman sitting so straight in her chair and the young one rising to escort him out. "Is there anything else, ma'am?"

"No, I think not. Thank you for humoring an old woman and coming so quickly."

When it appeared her attention had turned to the window, Dag bobbed his head and turned toward the door.

Clara, trying to determine what the undercurrents in the room meant, let him get ahead of her. Well of all the— again her mind found something to blame him for. Didn't he know it was *her* place to show him out? Her shoes tapped out her displeasure on the hardwood floor. How could she go around him? The hall wasn't wide enough. She glared at the back of the man. She'd have to find some new names to call him, the ones she'd used so far were wearing out!

Dag stopped at the head of the stairs. Clara did, too, with her nose in his back. Would he *never* do what she expected?

"Excuse me," she muttered, her head down to hide the blush she could feel flaming up into her face. She passed in front of him and preceded him down the stairs. Right now she could do with one of those fans she'd seen in a lady's book.

When she opened the door for him, she looked no higher than the missing button on his shirt. Wool underwear that might have once been white but had forgotten the experience long before showed through the gap of the shirt. Neither had had a recent acquaintance with a washtub.

Dag paused, as if to say something, then mashed his hat on his head, strode out the door, and down the walk.

Clara watched him stride away. For such a big man, he walked with the grace of. . .she couldn't think of a word. The picture of her father, head and shoulders above most of the Norwegian giants of home, whirling Mor around the dance floor in a spirited polka. Yah, Dag moved with that same grace. She corrected the thought, Mr. Weinlander. The bell summoned her from upstairs. She gently closed the door and made her way back up the staircase.

Thoughts of the curious bear of a man wriggled in and out of her mind as she continued with her tasks of the day. What would he look like without that matted rat's nest of a beard? Why wouldn't he talk with her, even to just the polite formalities? Why had her picture been on the table? Why didn't she just ask Mrs. Norgaard and get her questions answered?

That night as she prepared her charge for bed, Clara could feel the questions welling up and pleading for voice. After blowing out the lamp on the stand, she cleared her throat. Only the light from the hall disturbed the darkness.

"Would you repeat our Psalm again?" Mrs. Norgaard derailed Clara's train of thought.

"Yah, that I will." Clara sat down on the edge of the bed and closed her eyes. Her voice gentle, she began. "The Lord is my shepherd, I shall not want. . . ." As she continued, the words sank into her heart and mind, reminding her of the promises God wrote for everyone. When she finished, she bowed her head. Peace and quiet have the same sound, she thought. Why is it that words written so long ago have such power to bring peace?

"Our Father which art in heaven...." Mrs. Norgaard's voice with these other ancient words only added to the blanket of comfort. Clara joined her and together they whispered "Amen."

When Clara began to rise, Mrs. Norgaard laid a hand on the younger woman's arm. "Stay with me a while, if you will. I have a story I want to tell you." The words came softly out of the shadowed bed.

Clara settled herself with her back against the carved walnut foot. She waited.

"It all began a long time ago. A man here in town lost his wife one winter and left him with a small son. He had a hard time of it but eventually found another woman to marry. There has never been a surplus of marriageable females here in the Dakotas so he felt blessed. The family was fine until the new wife had a baby. All she could think of was her son, and the older boy was pushed aside.

"Now as the lads grew, the younger son was quick to learn. None could resist his laughing eyes and curly hair, least of all his mother. And so he grew to take advantage of his older brother, who was not so quick to learn or glib of tongue.

"When the older was ten, the father died, making his elder son promise to care for his stepmother and half-brother. They both treated him cruelly but he finally left school that, although he was slow, he loved, and he then took an apprenticeship under the local blacksmith. When the blacksmith died, he willed his business to the young man who had proven to have an amazing aptitude.

"And the younger son? Since his mother spoiled him so terribly, he felt that others should treat him like she did and drifted in with the wrong element of town."

"And of the older brother?" Clara forced the words past the lump clogging her throat.

"He continued to withdraw, caught, I believe, in a web of agonizing shyness, convinced he was not worth more than his family has repeatedly told him. And that was nothing.

"It reminds me of Esau and Jacob." Mrs. Norgaard sighed and a pause deepened. "I don't know, God worked a miracle for those two brothers of so long ago and I pray the same can happen today."

"You've prayed for them?"

"Oh, for years. The elder and I struck up a friendship back when he was a lad and was helping me in my garden. My Einer was much too busy in the bank to dig up the garden and help prune the trees. We never had children. Sometimes I wonder if God didn't trust us enough to take good care of them."

"Oh, no." Clara bit back any more of a response, afraid she would halt the flow of gentle and dreamy words.

"So I made it a habit to acquaint myself with the village children and help where I could. One of my girls attended teachers' school in Fargo and one young man has finished medical school. Doctor Harmon keeps hoping this young man will return to North Dakota where we need doctors so desperately." Silence again.

"I receive letters from others who have married and moved away. They all were so special to me, not that I spoiled them you know. I just made sure that if they wanted to do more with their lives, they could."

Clara drew a bit of flannel from her pocket and blew her nose. "And the younger brother?"

"I haven't seen him in a long time. Good riddance to bad rubbish, I say, but then I have to remember my Lord's commands and pray forgiveness both for my bad thoughts and his bad actions."

The clock chimed from the top of the six-drawer chest.

"You must go to bed now, my dear. Thank you for listening to an old woman's ramblings."

Clara bent over and brushed a kiss on Mrs. Norgaard's forehead. *"Mange takk."*

"God bless."

I have to help him, Clara lay in bed and stared upward at the canopy she could barely discern. *How can I? What can I do, he won't even talk to me?*

She waited for heavenly inspiration.

The clock chimed the quarter-hour.

An owl hooted out in the backyard.

"How, God, how?"

eight

Clara woke with the same thought.

As she hurried through her morning ablutions, she ignored the gray skies without and the gray cloud within. How could someone have mistreated a young boy so? Especially the woman who agreed to be his mother.

And what could be done now?

No wonderful solutions had come to her during the night. Was she expecting too quick an answer to her prayers? She brushed her hair, frustration lending vigor to her brush strokes. Mrs. Norgaard said she'd been praying for years...and nothing. The lilt had left her voice when she answered the summoning bell. Along with the snap in her step.

Shortly after dinner, the doorbell pealed. Clara wiped her hands on her apron and hurried down the paneled hall between the kitchen and the front entry. It was probably the doctor needing a cup of coffee during his daily rounds.

"Ingeborge!" Clara reached out to draw her guest inside and instead found herself enveloped in a hug that immediately made her think of Mor. "Come in, come right on in."

"I hope I'm not intruding. John agreed to stay home with the little ones while they napped and so here I am."

Ingeborge unbuttoned her coat and let Clara remove it from her shoulders and hang the heavy black wool on the coat tree.

"I'm afraid Mrs. Norgaard might be asleep. She had a busy morning." She led the way into the parlor. "I'll go see and be right back."

"No, I came to talk with you." Ingeborge took a seat on the brown velvet sofa and patted the surface beside her. "For you see, I have an absolutely marvelous idea and I need your help."

"Me?"

"Yes, I am thinking of starting a class to teach English to those Norwegians who just immigrated."

"Like me?" Clara put a hand to her chest.

"Yes." Ingeborge gave a bounce on the slippery sofa. "Wouldn't you love to be able to speak and read the language of your new country?"

"Yah, for sure that I would." A cloud dimmed the rising excitement in her eyes. "But how could I leave Mrs. Norgaard?"

"I think that can be arranged. I just kept thinking what a struggle Nora had had and I know many others feel cut off because they can't talk easily—"

"That's it!" Clara clasped her hands and buried them in her apron between her knees.

"What? Tell me what?"

"You said anyone who needs help with talking?"
Ingeborge nodded.

Clara turned to face her friend "Even though he—I

mean, they, might have lived around here all their lives."

"I hadn't thought to include someone like that but of course." Ingeborge's brow wrinkled in concentration.

"Dag Weinlander." Clara leaned against the back of the sofa. "Ingeborge, you are the answer to my prayers."

"I'm glad to hear that since you aren't making a lick of sense."

"What do you know of Dag Weinlander?"

Ingeborge rolled her eyes upward and pursed her lips. "Not a great deal, I must admit. He doesn't come to church or any of the town socials. Besides, I have never found him to be very friendly when I've met him anywhere. You know, in a town this size, everyone knows everyone else and all their business, too. But he seems a puzzle." She tilted her head to the side and studied her friend. "I take it you know more?"

Clara told her the story she'd heard from Mrs. Norgaard. At the end of the tale, Ingeborge removed a cambric bit from her bag and dabbed at the corner of her eye. "I had no idea. Oh, the poor, poor man." She paused, staring at the bit of fabric in her fingers. She nodded and looked up at Clara, a smile widening her lips as she spoke. "We'll just have to help him out, won't we?"

That Sunday at church, during the announcements, Reverend Moen invited all those who would like help with their English to meet at the church on Tuesday evening at six-thirty.

Ingeborge looked over the heads of her brood to Clara.

Their private smile acknowledged that others would be invited, too.

When Clara returned home, she hung up her coat and tripped lightly up the stairs. The closing hymn kept echoing in her mind so she sang along, "Blest be the tie that binds, our hearts in Christian love. . . ."

Mrs. Norgaard waited for her in the chair by the window. "I love to hear you sing and that song is one of my favorites. Maybe I'll soon be able to go to church again. I think I miss the music most of all."

"Yah, these folks, they sing good." She took the other chair. "He did it, Reverend Moen said the English class will begin on Tuesday."

"Good. Then our next step is to invite Dag here for me to tell him about the class. His shop is not open for business today, so the livery is where he'll be. After dinner if you would, walk over there with a message for me. Do we have any more of your apple cake? He seemed to enjoy that."

"No, but I could put one in to bake while I finish the dinner." Clara stood and barely refrained from skipping out the door.

Down at the livery stable a while later, Will came out at her call, rubbing the dust off his hands as he came. "C'n I help you, *frøken* Johanson?" His grin displayed a gap between his front teeth, besides showing his delight at her arrival.

"I hope so. Is Mr. Weinlander here?"

"He's at the forge. You need a horse or sumpin'?"

"No." Clara shook her head, a wistful smile betraying

her desire as she looked to the stalls. "Perhaps someday I'll ride again but for now, Mrs. Norgaard is asking for Da—Mr. Weinlander to come see her."

"Right away." Will touched a finger to his forehead and trotted back through the barn to the separate building facing the other street. Ringing sounds of hammer on steel announced that Dag was hard at work. The lad returned in a matter of seconds. "Said he'll be right over, soon's he finishes the piece he's working on."

"Thank you." Clara refused to recognize the letdown feeling the answer gave. Had she expected him to walk back with her? She paused a moment. "You know, there's fresh apple cake if you would like to come, too."

Will rubbed his mouth with grimy fingers. "That'd be right fine, Miss, but one of us has to stay here. There's a team comin' back."

"Maybe another time?"

"I'd like that."

Clara quelled the urge to walk slowly in case Dag might overtake her and instead hurried to prepare the tray and make fresh coffee.

Dag was more taciturn than ever, if that were possible, when Clara showed him upstairs. He answered each of her carefully thought out questions with a grunt or nothing at all. She shook her head as she left the room. Getting him to talk was perhaps going to be more of a challenge than she'd thought.

When Clara reentered the room carrying the coffee tray, it was obvious Dag didn't agree with Mrs. Norgaard. He sat with arms crossed over his chest, his jaw set like a snapping turtle.

"Just think about it, please," Mrs. Norgaard pleaded. "You would find it easier to deal with your customers if you spoke more fluent English."

"I have plenty of business." Hoarfrost shimmered on each word.

"Well." The old woman straightened her shoulders and shot him a look that would have melted steel. "Do what you must. All I ask is you give it some thought. Set that down here." She pointed to the table by her side.

Clara hazarded a glance at Dag after carefully positioning the tray so Mrs. Norgaard could pour. He didn't appear to be melting.

Dag watched her hands as she set down the tray. Each movement flowed with the grace of a half-grown wheat field dancing in the wind. Why should he go to an English class? Resentment chased good sense around in his mind. They talked about speaking but would the class include reading? He thought wistfully of newspapers and the books that graced the shelf at his mother's house. He could barely decipher Norwegian, let alone English.

Why had he been so slow in school? Maybe he was a dumb dolt like Jude said. Stupid and slow—and ugly as a troll. Yah, the trolls were big and strong, like him, and ugly.

He heard a voice as from a great distance.

"Mr. Weinlander, your coffee. And would you have some apple cake?" Her voice sang like the birds at courting time.

Two of his favorite aromas, coffee and cinnamon. He sniffed appreciatively and accepted the offered food. "*Mange takk.*" English, speak English, you dolt! Show her you can. But Clara doesn't talk English, the other side stated. He felt like his brain had become a battlefield.

"Will seems like such a nice young man."

Answer her! Dag choked on his apple cake. He coughed and took a swig of coffee that only made him cough more. When he could breath again, he leaned back in his chair. Sweat beaded on his forehead. He looked up at Clara expecting to see condemnation but all her blue eyes radiated was compassion.

A glance at Mrs. Norgaard left him reeling. Dag staggered to his feet. "I must go." He left the house as if the hound of Heaven bayed at his heels.

"Wait! Dag, wait!" He was at the gate before her cries penetrated the voices raging in his brain. He strangled the spires on the gate with shaking hands. He could hear her shoes tapping out her hurry.

"Here." She thrust a napkin into his hand. "I wrapped this for Will since he said he couldn't come with you."

Dag nodded without looking above her hands and fled out the gate.

"What are we going to do?" Clara asked that night as she brushed Mrs. Norgaard's hair in preparation for bed.

"First we pray and then we wait."

Clara sighed. "But—"

"No buts, my child. Our Dag has his own devils to work

out and only our Father can do that for him. But you and
I. . .well, I think we shall invite both Dag and Will for
supper. Wednesday would be a good night, don't you
think?"

Clara fell into bed, both restless and relieved. Waiting
was so hard but at least she had someone with which to
wait. Dag had no one. Her prayers matched her feelings—
confused.

Monday there was a letter for Mrs. Norgaard when Clara
went to mail hers to Mor and Far. Clara studied the
handwriting. If only she could understand English! On her
way back to the house, she went by the blacksmith's and
handed Will a note to give Dag. It was an invitation to
supper.

"Umm...ah..." Will stuttered. He looked from the note
to Clara, over his shoulder to Dag working at replacing a
wagon wheel rim and back to the note, his gaze darting like
sparks flying from the anvil.

"Is there a problem?" Clara could sense his hesitation
even if she couldn't have seen it.

"Ah, no." Will shook his head. "He can't stop what he's
doing right now or he'll have to start all over so I'll give
him this when he's done."

"Oh." Clara felt a stab of disappointment. More
waiting! "Well, all right then." She turned and walked
back to the big house, her shoulders hunched against the
bite of the north wind. As the postmaster had said, it
looked, felt, and smelled like a snowstorm was on the way.

The note, delivered later by Will and crudely lettered as if the writer had missed more school than he had attended, declined the invitation.

Mrs. Norgaard tapped the folded paper against her hand. "I have a question for you, Will, and I want an honest answer."

Will shuffled his feet, hat squashed between his two hands. "Yes'um."

"Who wrote this?"

Will wrinkled up his forehead, clicked his tongue, shuffled his feet again, and rendered his hat totally useless. "I did."

"Did Dag see my invitation?"

Will nodded. He rubbed his chin with one index finger.

This time it was Mrs. Norgaard's turn to nod. "Clara, why don't you take the boy down and give him a sandwich and maybe some of that apple cake if there is any left. Good day, young man. I hope to see you again soon."

"Yes'm. Thank you." Will bobbed his head and followed Clara out the door. By the time he'd eaten his fill, hard pellets of snow were dashing themselves against the window. He mashed his hat on his head and trotted down the walk, turned once to wave again, and then picked up his feet to hurry home before he froze.

Clara thought about the discussion upstairs as she cleaned up the kitchen. What was going on? And the letter that came. Would Mrs. Norgaard share that with her as she had the others? And on top of all that, what would be their next sally in the war on Dag Weinlander?

"Tomorrow I think I shall want to go downstairs for dinner."

Clara immediately thought of all the steps. How would they ever manage? While Mrs. Norgaard could now walk around her room, she hadn't left it in. . .in. . .Clara had no idea how long.

"I want you to go to the smithy in the morning, if the weather cooperates, and ask Dag to come to carry me down. If he refuses to join us for dinner, why then he can return to carry me back up."

Clara felt a chuckle bubbling up from her midsection. She tried to contain it but failed miserably. "Gladly," she answered when they could both talk again.

"Oh, Clara," Mrs. Norgaard said as the younger woman was leaving the room for the night. "That letter, it was from Mrs. Hanson. She'll be returning next week."

Clara felt like she'd been struck by a widow maker.

The feeling of doom persisted as she crawled into her bed. If Mrs. Hanson was returning, she could go back to the farm with Carl and Nora. Why didn't the thought please her? She'd only seen her sister once and that was at church since the move to town.

But what would she do for a job? And how could she help Dag when she would be so far out in the country? And what about the English classes? *God, are You sure You know what is going on here? How can I thank You when I am so confused? Everytime I think I have things under control or at least figured out, something changes. Please help me.*

"Why the long face?" Mrs. Norgaard asked when Clara brought in the breakfast tray. "The sun is shining; we can proceed with our plan."

Clara nodded and poured the coffee. She probably wouldn't be doing this for much longer. She walked over to the windows and drew back the heavy draperies. Sun refracted from the diamonds bedded in the inch of pristine snow covering the yard. How clean and pure everything looked. Snow frosted the black branches of the elm tree and bonneted the wrought iron fence posts. An unconscious sigh lifted her shoulders.

"All right. Out with it. This is a side of Clara I've never seen and I'm not sure I like it." Mrs. Norgaard set her coffee cup down with a snap.

Clara sighed again, this time fully aware of what she was doing. But sighing seemed all she was capable of at the moment. She turned to face her employer. "I just want to say how much I've appreciated working for you and—"

"Clara, what are you saying? Are you going to leave me?" Mrs. Norgaard pushed away the bed tray and made as if to rise.

"Well, the letter from Mrs. Hanson. If she's to come back. . . ."

Mrs. Norgaard flopped back against her pillows and patted her chest with one hand. "Oh, my dear, is that all? Why you silly goose. Did you think I would let you go just because Mrs. Hanson—oh, no, no, no. You have given me life again. I want you as long as you'll stay. Please, come here to me." She held out both hands.

When Clara took them, Mrs. Norgaard drew her young helper down on the bed. "Now, promise me if you are unhappy here, you will tell me."

"But I'm not. I just thought—"

"And that when you have concerns that trouble you, you'll bring them to me so we can work them out."

Clara nodded. The lump in her throat made an answer impossible.

"Good. Now that we have that all taken care of, what shall I wear for my first trip down to the dining room? I must look my best if we are to have company."

When the preparations were all complete, Clara threw on her coat, pinned her hat cockily over one eyebrow, and started out for the blacksmith shop. Her breath puffing out like miniature clouds delighted her as did the squirrel scolding her from the oak tree.

"I thought you'd be hibernating by now," she scolded back. "Go wrap yourself in your bushy tail and stay warm." She leaned over and scooped up a handful of snow, packed it, and fired it at the trunk of a tree where it splatted perfectly.

I'm staying, I'm staying, thank You, God. Thank You, thank You. "Praise God from whom all blessings flow. . . ." Her clear soprano voice rose on the puffs of air and joined the crunch of her boots in an aria of praise.

"To carry her downstairs?" Dag looked at her like she was missing a spoke somewhere.

Clara nodded, determined to keep a straight face. "She

can't manage the stairs yet but she so wants to be free from her bedroom for a change." She carefully injected a note of pleading into the last words. It *was* the truth.

"And then back up."

"After we eat."

"Tell her I will come to carry her down and back up." He slapped one hand into the other. "But no dinner."

Clara nodded. "At twelve then?" She caught Dag's nod as he walked off into the dimness of his shop. He *had* talked to her, at least. She allowed herself one skip on the way back home.

While Dag carried Mrs. Norgaard with a gentleness that belied his huge size, he refused to answer any of Clara's questions or comments. And he didn't stay to eat. The reverse process was no different.

"And tomorrow, Dag?" Mrs. Norgaard settled herself on the edge of the bed.

He nodded.

"Then I thank you. You have no idea what a treat this was. I think Clara's determination to make me live again is paying off, don't you?"

Dag nodded and set off as if that hound were on his heels again.

"I'm off now," Clara said from the bedroom doorway that evening. "You sure you'll be all right alone?"

"Perfectly. You just go and learn as much as you can." Mrs. Norgaard settled her spectacles more firmly on her nose. "I'm just grateful I can enjoy reading again." She waved her hand as if shooing away a fly. "Go on, go on."

Clara danced up the stairs a couple of hours later. She was learning to talk English! She and about fifteen other people. And Ingeborge, what a teacher. Everyone had had such a good time, why the hours passed like. . .like a party. She wrapped her hands around her shoulders and squeezed at the same time spinning in a circle.

"I take it you had a good time." Mrs. Norgaard laid down her book and removed her gold-rimmed spectacles.

"Yah. . .*nei*. . .yes. Good evening." The English words came haltingly but they came. "And we are to meet on Thursday, also." Clara switched back to Norwegian, having used up her store of new words. "Oh, I am so happy."

Wednesday and Thursday Dag appeared to do the carrying—but no eating.

On Friday, when Clara answered the door, she fought to keep the shock from showing on her face.

nine

Dag had washed himself—and his clothes.

Clara clamped her teeth together and made sure her cheeks spread in a smile. "Good morning." She hesitated over the words but persevered, determined to use her new language.

Dag nodded and started toward the stairs.

"Ahh." The word for coat totally left her mind. She reverted to Norwegian.

Dag paused, one foot on the bottom stair. He turned to face her. "Yah. *Mange takk.*" He shrugged out of his black wool, thigh-length coat and handed it to her.

Clara hung it on the tree and stared up the stairs. Even his boots were polished. What she'd give to see the look on Mrs. Norgaard's face! Clara ran up the stairs and down the hall. She burst into the bedroom just as Dag was leaning over to pick up his charge. His broad back hid the diminutive older woman from Clara's sight but when he turned around, Mrs. Norgaard just smiled like this was an everyday occurrence.

Clara stepped back and let them precede her down the hall. As they passed, Mrs. Norgaard winked at Clara, then continued her conversation with Dag. He even answered her question.

Clara leaned against the door frame and watched them disappear down the stairs. She clapped both hands to her cheeks and felt a shiver of pure delight course through her. She rolled her lips together, straightened her spine, and made her way downstairs.

Dag and Mrs. Norgaard visited in the sitting room while Clara quickly set another place at the table. After bringing in the bread she'd baked just that morning and the stew that had simmered for hours, she crossed the hall to announce the meal.

"No, I'll walk," Mrs. Norgaard insisted when Dag bent down to pick her up. "It's just the stairs I can't manage. Here, let me have your arm to lean on."

Dinner passed with Clara and Mrs. Norgaard carrying the conversation but Clara could feel Dag's gaze on her from time to time. He answered when asked a direct question but other than that, he ate in silence. Clara and Mrs. Norgaard made a point to discuss the English class taught by Ingeborge.

"We'll have our coffee in the sitting room," Mrs. Norgaard said after inserting her napkin back into the silver ring by her plate. Dag surreptitiously followed suit and leaped from his place to help her to her feet.

This became the pattern for the next three days until Saturday when Mrs. Norgaard suggested Dag help her down the stairs, rather than carrying her.

"You're sure?" He stared intently into her eyes.

"Clara's been making me walk around my room morning, noon, and night. You'd think she took lessons from an army sergeant."

"I'm just following doctor's orders." Clara defended herself.

"I know, my dear." Mrs. Norgaard smiled at her. "But you must admit you take your duties seriously."

Dag watched the byplay between the two women, aware as ever of the way they made him feel. Was this the way people really treated each other? He'd never heard or sensed a cross feeling between the two of them. Just a caring that flowed peaceful and smooth like the Red River on it's summer journey. And they extended that warmth to him. *Him.* Dag Weinlander. *Why?* Sure he had a strong back for carrying Mrs. Norgaard down the stairs but she had always made him feel welcome. Why?

Soon she wouldn't need him anymore. He thought of the gift he'd been carving for her in the evenings in front of the fireplace of his sod hut. Even that would help her need him less. The thought caused another pang in his chest. He kept his fingers from digging at the collar of his shirt.

Instead, he offered the old woman his arm, just like they did downstairs. She clutched his arm with both hands as she took the first step downward. He could feel her shaking. Another step. And another. When they reached the bottom, she gave a sigh of relief. His matched.

He swallowed and rubbed his mouth through the beard with one hand. Together, they marched directly into the dining room. After seating her, he sat down, refusing his body the privilege of slumping in the chair. That was worse than shoeing ten cantankerous horses in a row.

She let him carry her back up. "We'll see you tomorrow then. Dinner is at one, after Clara returns from church."

He nodded. "Oh, and Dag, please bring Will with you. I'd like to become better acquainted with that lad."

"Yes, ma'am." Dag turned to leave. "And *mange takk*."

"Dag, it is I who should be thanking you."

"Umm." Dag departed on that noncommittal reply.

That night he resanded the apple wood cane he had fashioned from a gnarled branch and applied a last coat of varnish. The twisted wood gleamed in the firelight as Dag set it aside to dry one last time. Each succeeding coat of varnish had deepened the patina, bringing out the highlights of the grain.

"That's beautiful," Will said from his stool by the fire. "When ya gonnna give it to her?"

"Tomorrow, when we go there for dinner."

"We?"

"Yah."

"Who's gonna tend the livery?"

"Me. While you heat water and take a bath."

"A bath! It's the middle of the winter."

"Yah, a bath." Dag ignored his assistant's fussing and put away his varnish and rag.

"I'd druther stay with the horses." Will crammed his hands into his pockets.

"You can, after dinner."

"What if someone needs a horse?"

"He can come back."

Will muttered his way to bed.

Dag remained by the fire, lost for a time in his thoughts. When he realized how many of those thoughts centered around a certain golden-haired angel, he abruptly stood and headed for the cornhusk-filled mattress he called bed.

"Dag, this is beautiful." Mrs. Norgaard rubbed her hands down the satiny finish of the cane. "I knew you were a master with metal but I had no idea you could create in wood, also." She gripped the handle and, standing, leaned her weight on the cane. "And the perfect height." She looked up at him with a smile crinkling the corners of her eyes. "Tired of carrying me around?"

Dag shook his head. "You're sure it fits? I could make it shorter if you want."

"No, this is perfect." She thumped it on the floor. "Now, shall we join the others downstairs?"

Dinner passed swiftly with Will finding time to answer questions in spite of putting away a prodigious amount of roast beef, mashed potatoes, gravy, and green beans.

"I ain't never had such a fine meal." Will leaned back against his chair.

"We have apple pie. I'd be sorry if you were too full to join us." Mrs. Norgaard smiled as she spoke.

"No'm. I'll find room for that."

Clara stood up to clear the table.

"I'll help you, miss." Will leaped to his feet. He grinned a cheeky grin. "That way I'll have more room for pie."

"Have you thought of joining the English class, Will?" Mrs. Norgaard asked when the coffee was poured and pie handed out.

"Naa. I can talk Norwegian, English, and some German. I don't need no class."

"But can you read English?"

"Pretty good. Pa made sure I went to school till I was eleven. Then we started west." He took a last bite of the pie.

"Where are your folks now?" Clara asked.

"Dead." Will scraped up every last bit of apple from his plate.

Clara wished she'd bit her tongue before asking such a question.

"Then Dag found me and asked if'n I wanted to help him, as an apprentice." He licked the tines of his fork.

Mrs. Norgaard motioned Clara to get the boy another piece of pie.

"I told Dag he should go—to that class, you know." He grinned at Clara when she set another slab of dessert in front of him. "Winter's a good time, not so busy. He could go."

Dag felt warmth creeping up from his chest and making his collar even tighter. Kicking the boy from under the table was beginning to seem more and more like a good idea. He'd never seen him so loose-mouthed.

Will looked across at his employer. He grinned again. "Could."

"We'd better get back in case someone needs a horse." Dag accompanied his pronouncement with the shoving back of his chair.

"*Mange takk* for my cane," said Mrs. Norgaard. She rose to her feet. "Perhaps just your arm today, helping me with the stairs." As they made their way slowly upward, she added a thought. "See you tomorrow?"

Dag nodded. "Yah." Was that gratitude for another day's reprieve he felt welling up in his heart? How terrible to wish she weren't getting better so quickly. Just like a dolt like you, he chastised himself with each upward step.

Mrs. Norgaard stopped three steps from the top. She put her hand to her heart and leaned against Dag's strength while trying to catch her breath again. When Dag made to lift her, she stopped him. "No, I'll make it. Just weaker than I thought." A pant separated each word.

See what you did? His inner tormentor continued. *You were in such a rush to get back to the barn, you. . . .*Dag clenched his teeth. *Would you never do things right?*

"Good afternoon," Clara practiced her English as she showed the men out. "See you at class Tuesday." She shut the door before Dag could answer.

Clara scoured the kitchen and polished all the furniture on Monday morning while the bread was rising. Mrs. Hanson would be arriving on the four o'clock train and she didn't want the housekeeper to find one thing not up to snuff. Ham and beans browned in the oven sending a delicious aroma throughout the house.

Dag sniffed appreciatively when he walked up the newly swept walk. While the sun tried to shine, high gray clouds kept drifting across it's warmth. A north wind nipped around the corner of the house and caused Dag to shiver. His hands were still cold from the scrubbing he'd given them in the horse trough. This cleaning up for dinner every day took some doing. He tucked a button back into its hole before ringing the bell. He'd have to buy some new clothes—and soon.

Clara answered the door while wiping her hands on her apron. "Good morning." The English was coming easier since she'd been practicing. "Come in."

Dag nodded and stepped inside, removing his coat as he did so and hanging it up himself. While his nose might be more accustomed to perfumes of horse, coke fire, and steel, he could recognize beeswax, lemon oil, and especially freshly baked bread with ham and beans. This, like every meal he'd enjoyed here, would be good—very good.

"See, I'm stronger every day thanks to you and Clara," Mrs. Norgaard stopped at the bottom of the stairs. She looked back up. "I didn't think I would ever leave that room again, except to greet my Lord in heaven."

Dag covered the small hand that lay on his arm with his large one. "I'm glad you decided to stay with us."

"As I said, thanks to you and Clara." She released his arm and set out with her back rigid but her weight partly supported by the apple wood cane clasped in her right hand. "See how well this works? Thank you, my friend."

Dinner indeed lived up to what his nose had promised him. He cleaned his plate and nodded when Clara offered to dish him up some more. "You are a good cook."

His comment caught the women by surprise. He never

offered anything except "*Mange takk*" unless spoken to first.

"Why, thank you," Clara answered, heat blossoming in her cheeks. "I. . .I wanted everything perfect for when Mrs. Hanson comes back."

Dag looked around at the gleaming furniture and his healthier friend and nodded. "It is."

Clara felt like she'd been given a medal by the King of Norway. Her heart pitter-pattered in her throat—her very dry throat. She blinked against the surge of moisture that should have been in her throat but instead wanted to slip from her eyes. "Thank you" seemed such an ineffectual response to so great a gift but what else could she do? "*Mange takk*," she replied.

"Take this to Will," she said as she thrust a package into his hands on his way out the door. "And. . . ," she gave him a saucy grin, "see you at class tomorrow night."

Mrs. Hanson clapped a hand to her chest when she saw Mrs. Norgaard sitting in the parlor, her royal blue bombazine skirt topped with a white, lace-tucked shirt-waist. Her mother's cameo glowed from it's position pinned to the high collar.

"Well, I declare, what has been going on here while I was off caring for my ma?"

Clara giggled behind her. "We wanted to surprise you."

"Lord love you, that you did." She walked over and stood in front of Mrs. Norgaard. "How'd you get down here?"

"I walked." She touched her cane and beamed at Clara. "With help, of course, but I shan't need that much longer. Doctor's prescription here in Clara has done it's marvelous work."

Mrs. Hanson sank down in a facing brown velvet chair. "Then you won't be needing the likes of me no more."

"Don't be silly. Now you sound like Clara when I told her you were coming home. I need and want you both. So unless you have another idea, that will be the last time we'll talk about such a matter." She thumped her cane for emphasis.

Clara and Mrs. Hanson swapped grins.

Mrs. Norgaard looked from the cane to their happy faces and chuckled herself. "Never thought of a cane as part of a conversation before."

In class that night, the students were practicing their greetings and farewells when the door opened and a big man walked in.

"Can I help you?" Ingeborge asked, then clapped her hands to her cheeks. "Dag Weinlander, is that really you?"

"Yah," he replied, nodding his freshly barbered head with neatly trimmed beard. The wild mass of stringy hair now lay on the cutting floor. Thick sable hair waved back from a broad forehead and ended just above his collar. A wide mouth with smiling lips split the beard that just covered his chin.

Clara noticed every detail. The way his ears lay close to his head and the richness of the waving hair. But what caught her attention the most were his eyes. No longer shrouded by clumpy hair and shaggy brows, eyes the blue of high mountain lakes on a summer's day stared back into hers.

She swallowed. She'd been attacked by dry throat again. "Hello, Dag," she croaked.

That night while Ingeborge was explaining the alphabet, Clara caught herself watching Dag. He didn't participate, but sat observing. He looked so different. From wildman to handsome. She couldn't wait to tell Mrs. Norgaard.

"I've been thinking," Mrs. Norgaard said over breakfast, and after they'd wondered at the change in Dag, "about ways to help you with your English. Now that Mrs. Hanson is back and I'm so much better, your duties will be of a different sort."

Clara stopped with a spoonful of hot cereal halfway to her mouth. She set the spoon back in the bowl. "What do you mean?"

"I know how hard you are trying with your English lessons so I have decided we will speak only English in this house. Mrs. Hanson and I agree. We'll help you, prompt you, whatever we can do but there will be no more Norwegian. What do you think?"

I think I'm going to throw up, Clara thought. She stared from Mrs. Norgaard to Mrs. Hanson and back again. "But, but...I...." She licked her lips. One of her favorite Bible verses from Chapter Four of Philippians floated through her mind. "I can do all things through Christ which strengtheneth me." She sucked in a deep breath. Her smile flickered like a candle in a draft and then steadied. "All right." She let her rigid shoulders slump. What on earth had she agreed to?

Thanksgiving passed in a daze for Clara. The English only rule applied when Dag and Will joined them for the annual feast. Will thought it was great fun, while Dag and Clara sneaked each other commiserating glances.

But Clara never felt persecuted. While discouragement sometimes dogged her, she knew they were all taking great pains to help her learn the language quickly. And it was working. With the daily repetitions, lessons with Mrs. Norgaard morning, afternoon, and evening, and her classes at the church twice a week, Clara could finally communicate.

She practiced on the shopkeepers, people at church, the postmaster. She talked to the woman in the mirror and dreamed of taking her new skill out to the Detschman farm.

All the while she spent learning English, she also prepared for Christmas. She fashioned a cloth baby doll dressed in a baptismal gown for Kaaren and sanded wooden blocks for baby Peder. While memorizing vocabulary words, she worked the hardanger lace for an apron for Nora. Mittens and a stocking hat for Carl could be knitted while she conversed with Mrs. Norgaard.

Her present for Mrs. Norgaard was the main problem. No one had found her a canary yet.

One night Dag walked her home from the church. "Won't you come in for coffee?" she asked, her English no longer halting on the simple phrases.

"Yes, thank you." While Dag sounded more stilted, he, too, followed the English only rule.

"Ah, welcome, Dag. Come in, come in." Mrs. Norgaard beckoned from her chair in the sitting room. "You know, I've been thinking...," she continued after the coffee was served.

Clara felt her stomach fall down around her knees. Everytime she heard "I've been thinking" from Mrs. Norgaard, their world turned upside down.

"I think you should come over every evening when there is no school and join us for extra work on English, both speaking and reading. And you could bring Will. I have a hunch he needs some help and is afraid to ask." She peered over her spectacles. "Or embarrassed. Not everyone is able to finish school, in fact, few are."

Dag stroked his chin. He stared right back at the woman across the room. "Yes."

"That's all?" Clara's voice squeaked on the last word.

"It won't be easy." Mrs. Norgaard continued her observation. "Nothing is."

Clara thought about that bald statement when she lay in bed that night. "Nothing is." Was that the way Dag's entire life had been? She thought to her childhood, to the laughter, the pranks, and even school. For her, learning was easy. Even this learning a whole new language was more time consuming than hard. But then, look at the people she had helping her.

She snuggled down under the covers. Now Dag would have those same people helping him. Plus her. She'd be glad to help. Would he be able to accept *her* help? She thought of the stubborn look on his face when he read aloud in class. If determination was all it took, Dag had it by the mountainful.

Each night as she said her prayers, she included him. After all, she'd promised to do what she could and if Mrs. Norgaard could pray for Dag all these years, could she do less?

Funny, lately she hadn't been praying for her curly haired husband-to-be. When she thought about it, several weeks had passed with him not even entering her mind.

"Please take care of him, wherever he is and whoever he is," she concluded. "Amen."

Several days later when Reverend Moen came to call, Clara stopped him in the hall and, in a low voice, asked him if he'd located a canary yet. At the shake of his head, Clara felt a moment of panic. Christmas was almost here and she'd been so sure she'd have a singing present for her friend.

"I'm sorry," Reverend Moen said.

"Me, too."

That evening Clara asked Dag to come into the kitchen with her while Will was settling down with his books by Mrs. Norgaard in the dining room.

"Do you know anyone who might sell a singing bird,"

she paused, trying to remember the word. "A canary. I will give this to Mrs. Norgaard for a Yule present so she has music in her life."

Dag nodded as she finished speaking. "Yah, yes," he caught himself, "I do. My mother raises canaries to keep her company. I will ask her."

Clara stared at him in amazement. "Can you do everything?"

"I will see about this." He reached out with one finger and touched her smiling cheek. When he pulled away as if burned, both he and Clara returned with all speed to the other room.

For the rest of the evening, her cheek felt hot to the touch, as if it had been fire that leaped between them.

The doorbell rang several days later. When Clara opened the door, she saw Will nearly buried under the green needles of a pine tree. "The train brought in a load of Christmas trees and Dag made sure you got the finest." He dragged it inside. "Where do you want it?"

"In the sitting room. We cleared out in front of the window. Mrs. Hanson brought up a bucket of sand from the cellar." Clara felt like a child again, dancing with excitement. She wanted to clap her hands and whirl around the room but instead she helped Will stand the tree up. "Oh, it is just perfect."

"There are more branches for you to decorate with but I couldn't carry everything at once." Will started to brush the needles off his coat but looked around, guilt flagging his already red cheeks.

"Let me take that for you." Clara helped him shrug out of his coat and took it outside to shake. By the time they had the tree set in the bucket, Mrs. Hanson had brought the decoration box down from the attic.

"I gotta be going." Will stared wistfully at the colorful balls and candle clamps in the box.

"Would you like to help us decorate the tree?" Mrs. Norgaard caught his look and asked.

Will nodded. "But I gotta get back to the stable. Dag needs me."

"That is fine. But both of you be here at six and tonight, instead of class, we'll pop popcorn and decorate the tree."

Joy sparkled in Will's eyes as he darted out of the room, returned to grab his hat and coat, and went plunging out the door. They heard his "Yee-haw" as he leapt off the porch and ran down the walk.

Dag hadn't looked her in the face since the night he touched her cheek. Clara frowned at the face in her mirror as she gave her golden hair a final brushing and swooped the sides back and up with her mother-of-pearl combs. What was she to do with him? After all, it was just a *touch*. She caressed the spot with her fingertips. And what was a touch between friends?

Should she mention it tonight while they were decorating the tree? She shook her head. No, better to act as if it never happened. She nodded and tried on a smile. A fingertip touched the place again. He had been so gentle. Like the kiss of a butterfly's wing. Her eyes flew open—

wide open—at the word kiss. She turned and ran from the room as if chased by...by the thought of hugs and kisses—and love.

The evening was an unmitigated disaster, as far as Clara was concerned. Dag never once spoke to her. He acted as if she were invisible. Clara lifted her chin higher and teased Will like she did her younger brother at home. She kept everyone laughing with her antics—all but the big man with the somber mountain lake eyes.

The tree, however, became the most beautiful she'd ever seen. Because she couldn't resist any more than a child, Mrs. Norgaard broke tradition and let them light the candles, just for a minute.

"Ohhhh." Their breath, expelled all at once, became a sigh of gratitude for something so lovely. The tree shimmered and sparkled, each glass ball and icicle refracting the candlelight and magnifying the glory.

As they pinched out the flames, the memory lingered, a preview of Christmas to come.

Clara and Mrs. Hanson spent the days baking. *Krumkake, fattigmanns,* and frosted sugar cookies. Clara took one day rising and kneading the sweet dough for *julekake,* the Norwegian Christmas bread, studded with currants and candied fruit and flavored with cardamom. The house smelled heavenly. And each evening, there were new goodies to share with her two fellow students.

Dag rapped on the back door early December twenty-fourth. He put his finger to his lips when Mrs. Hanson started to greet him.

"Is Clara here?" he whispered.

Mrs. Hanson nodded. "Come in and I'll get her. You want some coffee? Breakfast will be ready soon."

"I have the canary for her for Mrs. Norgaard."

Mrs. Hanson pressed her hands together in delight. "I'll get her."

Dag had returned with a quilt-padded bundle and was unwrapping it when the two women tiptoed into the room.

"How did you keep it warm enough?" Clara asked, reaching to help in the dismantling. At the bottom were several stones, still warm from the oven.

"Ma and I packed him real careful. She says he's one of her best singers."

Just then the bell pull from Mrs. Norgaard's room chimed. They started, like kids caught with their hands in the cookie jar. Mrs. Hanson clapped a hand over her mouth to stop the giggles. "I'll go see what herself wants. If I'm talking with 'er up there, she might not hear you." She turned back at the door, her eyes alight with excitement. "Like we talked, Clara, I think the furnace room is the safest place for him. It's warm and dark so maybe he won't sing."

"Ma says that sometimes when you move them like this, they don't sing for a while." Dag removed the last cloth. A bright gold canary cocked his head and looked the two of them over. He cheeped and hopped down from his perch, then up to the sides of the cage, all the while watching his observers. He cheeped once or twice and then attacked the seeds in his dish.

"He's beautiful." Clara clasped her hands together. "Do you think she'll like him?"

"I'm sure she will." He began folding the quilts. "I brought a bag of seed and Ma says you can sprout some for him in the windowsill. He like greens sometimes and fresh water."

"How much do I owe you?" Clara couldn't take her eyes from the bit of sunshine hopping around the cage.

"Nothing."

"But Dag. . . ."

He picked up the cage and turned toward the cellar door. "Maybe we should put a lamp down there with him for a time, just to keep him company."

"But Dag, this is my present to give."

"Just include Ma in it. She was pleased to be able to return a favor."

"And you. Without you I wouldn't have found him." Clara looked up into the face of the man towering over her. Why was it that she felt both safe and. . .and. . . . She put her hand on Dag's. "Thank you, my dearest friend." Warmth flowed up her arm and curled in the pit of her stomach.

"Ah, good." Mrs. Hanson said as she reentered the room. "I'll check on the bitty thing every hour or so. This is turning into the best Christmas this house has seen in years. Hurry with that and we'll all eat together. Clara, help Mrs. Norgaard get ready and Dag, you can bring herself down as soon as she rings."

Clara flew up the stairs to help Mrs. Norgaard with her toilet.

"Who is that downstairs?" the old woman asked.

Feeling caught, Clara stuttered. "D-Dag."

"What did he want so early in the morning?"

"Ah-h-h." Even a little fib was outside Clara's capabilities. She resorted to the ruse her parents always used. "You shouldn't ask questions. Remember, this is Christmas."

"I'm not about to forget with all the secrecy that's been hatching around here." Mrs. Norgaard tried to look stern but failed miserably.

The weather held fine for Christmas Eve so Clara hoped her sister and her family would be able to attend the service. Dag promised to bring a sleigh so Mrs. Norgaard could attend, also. This would be her first time in church since her illness.

"Are you sure going out won't lay you low again?" Mrs. Hanson asked quietly, but Clara heard the exchange.

"No, I am fine in health and thankful for this my new family since this will be the first Christmas without my Einer."

Clara started. In all the excitement, she hadn't thought about Mrs. Norgaard's feeling sad. No wonder she had been more quiet lately.

"But this huge house needs lots of people like this coming and making Christmas right. We need little children here. We must invite the Moens, they have no family in town either."

They were gathered in the hall when the jingle of harness bells announced the arrival of the sleigh. When they stepped out the door, the cold bit their noses and cheeks but Dag soon had them all swaddled in robes, right up to the tips of their noses.

Once out on the street, Clara looked up to see the stars hanging low and brilliant in a cobalt sky. "Oh, look." She pointed to the north. Aurora borealis, the Northern lights, danced on the horizon, flaring reds, blues, and greens in an unending heavenly display.

"Only God could create something so magnificent," Mrs. Norgaard whispered. "And to think He brought them out tonight just for me to see. Only He knows how much I have always loved the Northern lights."

When they entered the church, the heavenly chorus from outside seemed to follow them in. Clara found herself sitting between Dag and Will, right behind Nora and her family. Ingeborge turned from her place in the front pew and wiggled her fingers. The old familiar hymns soared to meet the stars and the reading of the Christmas story settled into every heart.

When Dag shifted on the words, "Peace among men with whom he is pleased," Clara slipped her hand into his. He stilled immediately. Wasn't that what friends were for, to help each other out?

She could feel him looking at her. The heat bathed her cheeks like a furnace had just been lit. She stared straight ahead, concentrating on the sermon.

As they stood for the final hymn, their hands touched, holding the hymn book. When she allowed her glance to travel up to his face, he stared back—and smiled.

Silence fell after Reverend Moen pronounced the benediction. A silence deep and full with the promise of Christmas. As they turned to leave when the organ swelled in triumphant joy, Doctor Harmon made his way to Clara's side.

"Clara, I hate to ask this, but I have a sick family with no one to help. Could you come?"

ten

"But my family."

"I know and this is your first Christmas in this land but I'm afraid if I don't have help, the Ahmundsons won't see another Christmas."

"I could go," Mrs. Hanson volunteered.

"Thank you, but someone younger and stronger could help me more. Besides, Clara seems to have that healing touch."

"I will go." Dag's strong voice came from beside and above her.

"Thank you, Dag. I can use you both."

"We will save the presents until you come back." Mrs. Norgaard patted Clara's arm.

"And the dinner." Mrs. Hanson nodded her head, setting the rose on her hat to bobbing.

Everyone seemed to be making the decision for her. Clara felt trapped, like she had no choice. She looked back at the altar, the golden cross shimmered in the candlelight. He, too, was telling her to go.

Clara turned to the doctor. "I am ready." She reached across the pew and hugged Nora and the children.

Carl shook her hand. "We will come for you when you have finished. Then we will all celebrate our Christmas."

"Go ahead like we had decided," Clara whispered to Mrs. Hanson. "I just won't be there to hear it's first song."

They dropped off the other passengers and followed Doctor Harmon and his cutter out of town. Only the jingle of bells and harness and the snorting of the horses broke the stillness of the midnight air.

The stench of illness smote them in the face when they opened the door to the farmhouse. They found the mother collapsed on the floor beside the cradle of her dead infant.

Dag fired up the stove as soon as they had the woman in bed beside her delirious husband and soon had warm water so Clara could bathe the sweating bodies.

"Give them as much water as you can get them to drink and keep sponging their bodies to break the fever." Doc glanced at the cradle. "I'll take care of that one later, when we have time. I brought onions to make a poultice, see if we can't help them to breathe easier. Soon's the stuff's cut up and steamed we can apply it. Mr. Ahmundson needs it the most."

Clara listened with one ear while she moved from bed to bed checking on the five children. Only one was cool to the touch and sleeping normally. "Let's move this one to a bed by himself," she suggested. "He's either had a light case or not sick yet."

Dag tenderly lifted each of the children while Clara changed the filthy beds and bathed the dehydrated bodies. When the littlest girl cried out and thrashed around in her agony, Dag crooned a little song that reached her fevered brain and let her relax. Working together, Dag and Clara were able to accomplish their tasks much more quickly.

The three of them worked through the night and the next day, taking turns sponging hot bodies, forcing water between parched lips, and collapsing on the spare bed when there was a moment. One by one, the children cooled, slept, and awoke. Only the parents suffered on.

Dag and Doctor Harmon both took time the next day to check on other patients and the livery. Clara dragged herself around, caring for the children and keeping the parents as comfortable as possible. At three the next morning the father passed the crisis and slipped into an easy healing sleep.

"Thank you, Father." Clara dropped down by the bed, resting her head on her hands. "Please" and "Thank you" had been her litanies for the last few days.

Dag returned in the morning with a kettle of soup, another of chicken broth, and clean sheets for the beds. He sent Clara to bed and took over the care again.

When Clara awoke in the afternoon, the mother was tossing from side to side, mumbling and calling for her baby. Mr. Ahmundson slept in a chair by the fire, a towheaded three-year-old asleep on his lap.

"Thank you, miss," he muttered, clutching her hand. "You're an angel for sure, come to save my family. Thank God for ye."

Clara patted his hand and headed back to her post beside the mother.

"She seems quieter when you are here with her," Dag

stood to let her have the chair. "Doc said he would be back later tonight. He thinks the crisis will come soon."

Clara could hear Dag in the other room, setting out bowls of hot soup for those well enough to come to the table and feeding those who couldn't. Neighbors had come in to do the chores, she heard him tell Mr. Ahmundson. Clara continued dripping spoonfuls of water between the mother's lips and sponging her heat-ravaged body.

"You go get some sleep," the doctor said when he returned late in the evening. "I'll watch with her now."

Clara shook her head. "I can't." She nodded to where the frail woman clutched her hand. "She needs me."

The candle flickered and died and Doc went into the other room to find another. Clara could feel death hovering in the corner. Prickles chased each other up and down the back of her neck, making her afraid to look in case she should see his face.

"No!" She gritted her teeth. "Father, hear us. Her children need her. Please, come with Your Spirit and breathe life into her body."

The woman's breath grew fainter. The exhalations farther apart.

Clara breathed for her, with her. With each intake she whispered, "Live" and with each sigh, she called on the name of our Father.

Mr. Ahmundson stirred from the chair on the other side of the bed where he had drifted off. Tears ran down his sunken cheeks as he took her other hand and pleaded. "Don't leave us, my Inge. Please come back, we need you so."

"Come on, you must fight to live." Clara wanted to jump to her feet and pound her fists on the wall. Instead, she smoothed the cool cloth over Inge's forehead again and down the sides of her face.

"You must let her go," the doctor said softly.

Clara shook her head. She laid her face down on the woman's hand and let the tears bathe the dry skin. "Go with God, Inge." The woman's hand twitched in hers. Clara could hear a breath, a shuddery breath, and a long pause.

Inge breathed again and then again. Her breathing steadied and a slight smile touched the corners of her mouth.

"She's sleeping. Thank the good Lord, He brought her back." Doctor Harmon gripped Mr. Ahmundson's shoulder. "She's turned the crisis."

Clara sank down on her knees beside the bed. This time tears of joy helped cool the hand she held. "Thank You, Father, thank You," she repeated over and over. When she looked in the corner, all she saw was a dress hanging on a hook.

The first thing Clara heard when she returned home a couple of days later was the trill of a canary. She followed the song to the sitting room where Mrs. Norgaard sat in the window reading her letters. Mrs. Hanson occupied another chair, her knitting basket at her feet and turning the heel on a gray wool stocking.

"Child, you're back." Mrs. Norgaard rose to her feet so swiftly, her letters scattered across the floor. "Come, sit down. Mrs. Hanson, the coffee. Are you all right?" Her words ran over each other in her haste.

"Oh, isn't he beautiful?" Clara stopped in front of the cage where the small gold bird with a patch of black on his wing eyed her from a beady eye. She continued over to be enveloped in a hug that left no doubt of her welcome. "And yes, I am fine. Just tired."

"Have you eaten?" Mrs. Hanson joined them, alternating between patting Clara's shoulder and removing her coat and hat.

"Thank you, my dear, for my songster. He woke us on Christmas morning with a trill of joy. Our Savior is born and even the birds rejoice." Mrs. Norgaard leaned toward the cage and made chirping noises. The little bird cocked his head and responded in kind. "I think he would talk if he could."

Mrs. Hanson appeared with a coffee tray and set it on the glass-topped coffee table. "The soup's warming and after you get something filling in you, you're going up for a wash and bed. You look like you haven't slept for a month of Sundays." Mrs. Hanson bustled them both over to the couch and had coffee cups in their hands almost by magic.

"Dag told us how you cared for the Ahmundsons. Doctor Harmon says that without you, he'd have lost half the family."

"I saw death hovering the corner, black and ugly." Clara shuddered in remembrance. "But God's love drove him

back. I don't know, I've heard stories like this but. . . ."
She paused. "Inge says she heard us calling her so she
came back. It was so hard to tell her the baby had died. You
can't imagine how those poor people lived. Your soup
made all the difference." She patted Mrs. Hanson's plump
hand after accepting a steaming bowlful herself.

"It was them grasshoppers that did it for the farmers.
They ate everything showing above the ground. Vile
things." Mrs. Hanson shook her head, her tongue clicking
in time.

"What can be done for them?"

"You just get some rest and leave that to us." Mrs.
Norgaard said firmly.

Clara slept for two days, only rising for the necessary
bodily functions. When she made her way downstairs
after dressing after a bath in the hip tub, she heard voices
in the sitting room. Following the trail of both masculine
and feminine voices, she found all the chairs occupied.
When she smiled at the folks gathered, she realized all the
leaders of the town were gathered.

"Times are hard all over," the postmaster was saying,
"but like you said, Mrs. Norgaard, we got to take care of
our own. I got me a deer last week, I can put in that. And
a sack of flour. Martha says we got extra spuds, too. Some
reason those thievin' 'hoppers missed our place."

Clara felt tears sting behind her eyelids as everyone
around the room listed what they could share.

"We'll deliver things on Saturday, then." Dag looked
to Reverend Moen for confirmation. "From the church.

You and Doc know who needs supplies the worst?"

Reverend Moen nodded. "The ladies'll get together and break the sacks down into smaller pieces so's there's some for everyone."

"We'll take the coal out Friday. You say we have three tons, right?"

"So far." Reverend Moen consulted a list he held in his hand. "We can always use more of everything so pass the word along. As Christ said, 'Whatever you do for the least of these my brethren, ye do it onto Me.'"

Clara thought to the account at the bank where she had been saving her earnings. It would pay for bags of beans or whatever they needed the most. Were Nora and Carl some of those in need? Wouldn't her sister have said something if they were going hungry?

When she mentioned her concerns later to Mrs. Norgaard, the older woman shook her head. "No, Carl wasn't wiped out like others of the farmers, even though he was stripped."

"How do you know?"

"I own the bank, remember?"

"Oh." Clara chewed on the tip of her finger. "I guess I knew Mr. Norgaard owned the bank but when he died, I. . . ."

"Who else could he leave it to? We have no children and his brother died before he did. I have a good manager and now that I am feeling back to par, I will be more involved." Mrs. Norgaard leaned forward on her cane. "But let me tell you, the men of the town aren't too happy about having a woman at the helm of the bank." The three chuckled together.

The belated Christmas celebration was more than Clara
ever dreamed possible. The Detschmans sleighed into
town and the Moens walked over after church. Dag and
Will joined the group and Mrs. Nogaard's wish of children
laughing in her house came true.

There were presents for everyone. Toys for the children
along with dresses for the girls and pants and shirts for the
boys.

"How did she get the right sizes?" Ingeborge asked
Clara during the middle of the melay.

"I'll never tell." Clara smiled at her friend.

Ingeborge stroked the heather gray, fine wool shawl
she'd found in a package with her name. "I've never had
anything so grand."

"You had something to do with all this," Nora said, after
snagging Peder back from pulling himself up on the
Christmas tree.

Clara just smiled. Never had she shopped and spent
money like those last few weeks before Christmas. Since
Mrs. Norgaard couldn't manage the streets yet, everything
not ordered from a catalog had come home under the steam
of either Clara or Mrs. Hanson.

"Thank you, AuntieClara," Kaaren whispered, leaning
against her aunt's knees. "You made my doll good. I call
her Clara."

The lump that was never far away took up residence in
Clara's throat again. She watched Dag's eyes open wide
when Mary Moen handed him another package. When he

read the tag, he looked over at Clara, his face inscrutable.

She watched him finger the muffler she had knitted out of wool to match his eyes. Those eyes had an uncharacteristic shine when he looked at her again.

There was one red-wrapped package left. Mary brought it over to Clara. Slowly she opened the box. Inside she found a white leather-bound Bible. When she opened it, the words were all in English. The front fly read, "From your friend, Dag." She raised her gaze to meet his. The shine matched in both pairs of eyes.

By the time everyone had devoured the feast the women had prepared and gathered their presents, dusk crept over the land.

"We must be going," Carl said, gathering up his brood. "Thank you for the wonderful party and all the presents. We will never forget your goodness." He shook Mrs. Norgaard's hand and put the other around the shoulder of his wife. "Who could know when we waved goodbye to Clara what wonderful things would come of it."

Nora hugged her sister. Clara felt like she'd had a piece of home as they embraced. "I'll try to come out more often," Clara whispered in Nora's ear. "I have so much to tell you."

"And the man in the picture?"

Clara shrugged. "Who knows." *And who cares*, she thought.

The winter months passed quickly with evening classes both at church and at the house. Clara was called to help sick families several times and, each time, she prayed for those ill as much as she cared for their physical needs. Each time she was gone, she looked forward to telling Dag about her experiences upon her return.

One night after she returned from a week of caring for a woman with a newborn, she entered the house to find Dag in his usual seat at the dining room table, splitting his concentration between the book he studied and the page of sums he worked over. Mrs. Norgaard, hand on Will's shoulder, was explaining something to him and he with his usual grin, was making her laugh.

Slowly and quietly, so as not to bother anyone, Clara unwound her muffler and removed her coat. Was that a frown on Dag's broad brow? He concentrated so hard, not wanting to waste a moment now that he'd rediscovered the joy of learning. Her fingers itched to smooth the frown away.

Clara stared at her finger tips. What were they thinking of? She shifted her gaze to the man on the far side of the table. Sensing her attention, he raised his head. A smile broke forth that lighted his eyes and showed the gleam of his teeth.

Clara felt her heart clench in her chest. When it started beating again, the warmth spread clear out to the tips of her fingers and toes.

"Clara, you're home." He bounded to his feet and with him came all the others to welcome her back. When he took her hand in his, she felt a jolt clear up to her shoulder.

The memories kept her awake once she finally found her

bed. They were friends, good friends, she and Dag. There was no problem with that—was there? But what if what she felt was more than one would feel for a good friend—a male, good friend, a handsome male, good friend.

But what about the man in the picture? a small voice niggled at the back of her mind. Aren't you supposed to marry him—whoever he is? Wherever he is?

Dag strode home that night, his hands locked behind his back, shoulders hunched. He could still feel the jolt like lightning that coursed up his arm. What was he thinking of? No woman, especially not an angel like Clara, would want to love him. Love, there could be no love in his life. Only worthy men found love, and he, Dag, was the most unworthy of all.

You must not see her again, he ordered himself. But the thought of no more lessons, no more sightings of her smiling face, no more Clara beat him downward like a load of steel on his back. He couldn't do it.

You must! The inexorable voice pounded his brain and heart.

Warm chinook winds melted the snow and, with the kiss of the sun, green blades popped up almost overnight. Clara strolled down the street on her way to the post office and then to the general store. Two men on horseback raised their hats in greeting as they passed her.

Clara felt punched in the stomach. One of them, the one mounted on the striking palomino, was the curly haired man in her picture. She spun around to get a second look and saw him glance back over his shoulder at the same time. It was him. Absolutely.

Forgetting the errands, she picked up her skirt and once out of sight of the main street, raced toward the house. She stopped to unpin her hat that was flopping in a most decidedly unladylike manner and took off again. When she reached the porch, she clung to the white pillar.

Whew, she patted her pounding chest and tried to catch her breath. What she needed was a race or two up the mountains with her brothers.

"Clara, are you all right? What is wrong?" Mrs. Norgaard crossed the porch and stood in front of the panting girl.

"I'm fine. But. . .but. . . ." Clara sucked in a deep breath and forced herself to stand still. "I saw him!"

"Who?"

"The man in my picture. He just came riding into town. He's here! Right here in Soldall."

"Oh, no." Mrs. Norgaard paled and clutched her cane with both hands.

eleven

"He's already married," said Mrs. Norgaard.

"But he can't be. He sent me a ticket to come here, and his picture. Why would he do that if he were already married?" Clara found it difficult to breathe around the boulder sitting on her chest.

"I don't know."

"You know him then?"

Mrs. Norgaard nodded.

Clara swallowed. "You knew who it was when I showed you my picture?"

The old woman nodded again.

"And you didn't tell me."

"No, child. I knew he was no good and since nothing came of it, I hoped he would never return." Mrs. Norgaard turned back toward the door. "Come, let us sit and talk about this thing."

Clara looked up at the sky. Yes, the sun *was* still shining. Then why did everything seem so dark?

"Nothing has changed, you understand." Mrs. Norgaard continued when they were sitting knee to knee on the couch.

"But it has!"

"No. Now think about this. When you didn't know who

159

he was—"

"I still don't," Clara interrupted.

The older woman ignored her. "When you didn't know who he was, you went right on building a good life for yourself here."

"But I'm not married. I came to America expecting to be married."

"Yes, but think of your life in the last several months. Would you not have all that's gone on? You have good friends, you speak English well, you can read the language, you have literally helped keep people alive or brought them back from near death."

"No. Yes. I don't know. Does it have to be one or the other?" Clara fought back the tears that threatened to blind her. Here she'd been so excited and now all was ashes. "I thought maybe he was coming for me."

Mrs. Norgaard shook her head, clucking her tongue in sympathy.

"At least tell me his name, if you know it."

Mrs. Norgaard paused. She lowered her gaze to their clasped hands. "His name is Jude."

"Jude. Jude! As in Judas?" Clara threw herself against the back of the couch. "If that isn't poetic justice. Now I really understand what betrayal means." She looked up to catch a look of consternation cross Mrs. Norgaard's seamed face. "I think I'll go up to my room for a while. Don't call me if a certain young cowboy comes calling."

As she fell across her bed, she let the tears come. All of a sudden her life seemed in pieces when but a short while ago she was glorying in the signs of spring. Betrayed! She'd been betrayed. But what was the purpose behind all this? After all, a ticket from Norway to North Dakota cost a great deal of money.

As her brain began functioning again, the tears dried up. Now she vacillated between anger at a man who would do such a thing—to a person he didn't even know—and curiosity. Why? She got up and, sitting down at the dressing table, began brushing her hair. The soothing action always made her think better.

She took out the picture and the stained letter and tried to read them again but to no avail. Even knowing the man's name, the faded script made no sense. She studied the smiling mouth and laughing eyes. How could one who looked so. . .so. . .charming, was the only word she could come up with, do such a terrible thing?

After washing her face, she made her way back downstairs. She still hadn't finished the errands. Maybe she'd stop by the blacksmith's and talk to Dag for a bit. He always made her feel better.

Clara walked the way of the blacksmith's first. As she drew closer she heard two men laughing but neither laugh belonged to Dag or Will. The ring of hammer on metal continued unabated.

Hesitant to interrupt if Dag were conducting business, Clara paused outside the rolling door.

"So ya picked that bitty gal from Norway up at the station like I tol' ya."

"Jude, what are you talking about?" Dag's voice held

more than a note of exasperation. He spoke in English.

"Wal, looky here. My brother done learned to talk like ever'body else whilst I was gone."

Metal whanged on metal.

"So, did she think you was gonna marry her? Only the picture I sent didn't match what she see'd?"

Clara felt her eyes widen. She clamped her teeth on her lip to keep from crying out.

"You are not making any sense. I took Miss Johanson out to the Detschman farm like you asked and that was the end of it."

"But I sent 'er a letter, with my picture. Only I signed yer name."

"She'da thought you was to marry her." The second man spoke up for the first time.

Clara listened to the two men laughing hysterically and thumping each other on the back. She could feel Dag's pain, emanating from the building like the tolling of the bell when a fire broke out.

"Jude, just get out of town." His voice sounded flat, beaten.

"You low-down, rotten excuse for a human being." Clara flew around the corner like a banty hen defending her brood from a low-flying chicken hawk. "Anyone who would do such a cruel and spiteful thing to another—least of all his brother. Why you ought to be horsewhipped." She stood toe to toe with the tall man and shook her fist in his face. "You think you're so smart. You don't know what it is to be a man. Even the lizards know more about human decency than you do."

Jude backed away, flapping at her with his hands.

Clara met him, stride for stride. "Dag Weinlander is one of the finest men in the country. And you have the nerve to make fun of him. Why he's worth ten of you. Twenty or forty!"

"Lady, enough. Back away before—"

"Before you what? You take to beating women, too? And children I suppose. I pity your poor wife. God bless her to put up with the likes of you." She backed him all the way to his horse that also shied away from the barrage of verbiage.

Jude and his cohort swung aboard their mounts and hightailed it out of there. Jude looked over his shoulder as they fled, as if afraid she might pursue them farther.

"Thank God I didn't marry him!" Clara stamped her foot and dusted her hands together, as if good riddance to bad rubbage. As the dust settled, the enormity of what she had done began to seep into her consciousness.

She turned around to find Dag watching her, the old spirit of unworthiness beating him into the dust.

"That's the way! Miss Johanson, you done good." Will leaped forward to grab her hand.

"Will!" The tone of Dag's voice stopped the youth short. He turned, caught the nod, and, after giving Clara a hint of smile for encouragement, left to the recesses of the livery.

Clara watched the lad go and wished she could do the same. What must Dag think of her? She left off memorizing her shoe and looked up to catch the sorrow in her friend's face.

"Clara, how could you. . .?"

"How could I what?" She felt the force flow through her again. He believed what his conniving brother had said. After all these months, the old Dag was just waiting to be beaten again—by his brother. "Dag Weinlander, I'm amazed at you! Don't you know what a fine man you are? Everyone in town says so. Mrs. Norgaard thinks of you almost like a son. God made you to walk tall like the man you are. He doesn't make mistakes. God loves you and—" She bit off the words. She put a hand to her mouth. She'd almost said, "And so do I."

"And. . .and He wants you to be happy." She stared up at the face above her, drowning in the eyes of mountain lake blue. Eyes that had once clothed her in warmth but were now rimmed with frost. What had she done?

Clara turned heel and strode swiftly down the street before the tears she fought could win the battle.

Go after her, man, screamed the voice in his head. But Dag stood, as if rooted to the spot like a century old pine tree. What could he say? What could he do?

Clara, she was magnificent. He rubbed the inside of his cheek with the tip of his tongue. Never had he seen his brother back down and run off like that. Why, he'd been almost afraid to get in the way in case she turned on him. A chuckle tickled his ribs.

He picked up his hammer from beside the smoldering forge but instead of cranking the blower to heat the coals, he slipped the sledge into it's assigned slot on the work bench and sank down on an up-turned bucket.

Why didn't he let Jude have it? Why couldn't he think of a thing to say? He scrubbed at his scalp as if to drive the ideas either into his brain or drag them out.

Jude hurt Clara! The thought flared forth in a burst of pure, red rage. His brother tried to make a fool out of the woman he loved. Dag ground his teeth together. Where could he find him? He rose to his feet and began pacing back and forth. What would Jude do? Go home to their mother? Dag shook his head.

Hide out? He nodded. One fist slammed into the palm of the other hand. The rhythm beat with each stride. Where would the dirty dog hide? Step, slap. Would Clara ever speak to him again? Step! Slap! What difference did it make? Who was he that she should care?

He leaned against the support post, barely restraining himself from pounding his head against the wood. Dolt. Dag the Dolt. He heard again the jeering voice from his youth. One tear squeezed past the power of his will and trickled down into his perfectly trimmed beard.

When Clara returned to the big house, she dropped the mail on the hall table and dragged herself up the stairs. Without speaking to anyone, she staggered into her bedroom and slumped on the bed.

Dag, her best friend, would probably never speak to her again. And his brother—oh, she could wring his neck with her bare hands, just like butchering a mean, tough old rooster. But Dag—how could she stay in the same town and not see him. Not talk to him. Not study with him, laugh with him, see the world through his magnificent eyes. Not tend the sick or visit the well.

Her hand over her eyes blotted out the sun streaming in the windows.

When Mrs. Hanson knocked on the door, Clara sent her away with a mumbled excuse. What kind of a woman was she to scream at a total stranger like that? But he—Jude— what a perfect name for him—the betrayer—he had laughed at Dag. Tried to make a fool of him. Treated him like pond scum.

She bit her lip so hard she could taste the blood.

"God, Father, what am I to do?" The tears trickled down the sides of her face and watered her hair.

This must be how a bucket feels coming up from the well, she thought, as she pulled herself hand over hand toward the light. A rapping penetrated her fog. And repeated.

She forced open her eyes. The afternoon sun had dimmed to dusk. The thumping she now recognized as Mrs. Norgaard tapping on the door.

"Clara, dear, let me come in. I know you are in there." She tapped again.

Clara pushed herself up on her elbows. Had she locked the door in her anger? She shook her head. Waves sloshed from side to side within her skull. She groaned and flopped back down.

"Clara, please."

"Come in, it's not locked." She covered her eyes with

one arm to still the pounding in her head. She must look a sight. She could barely open her eyes they were so swollen.

Mrs. Norgaard pushed open the door and swept across the carpet. After studying the form crumpled on the bed, she sat down on the edge. "Is it really as bad as all this?" Her voice floated like dust motes on a warm and caring sunbeam.

Clara nodded. She clamped her fingers against pounding temples.

"I've taken the liberty of asking Mrs. Hanson to make you some sassafras tea. When she comes I want you to drink it all. Better than laudanum to ease a headache." She sat there, not moving.

Clara lay there, listening to her own breathing—and the blood pounding clear to her finger tips.

Even Mrs. Hanson was quiet, tiptoeing in and keeping her voluminous comments to herself. She set the tray down, light as a whisper and, after propping Clara against pillows stacked and fluffed behind her, left the room.

"Here." Mrs. Norgaard handed Clara the cup as soon as the young woman opened her eyes.

Clara took a sip and made a face.

"Drink it, it's good for you."

Clara obeyed, her thoughts and feelings in too much of a muddle to resist.

When the pain lines furrowing Clara's forehead relaxed, Mrs. Norgaard settled herself in a chair she'd pulled over to the bed. "Now, my dear, I can't help you unless

I know what terrible thing has transpired."

"I'm so ashamed." A sob turned into a hiccup.

"What could you have done to make you so ashamed?"

Clara waited, wishing the woman would disappear on one hand and that she were a mind reader on the other. Then she wouldn't have to tell the entire miserable tale.

"There I was, screaming like fishwife, right out where half the town could hear."

Bit by bit, Mrs. Norgaard dragged the story from her sorrowing friend.

"And so, Dag will probably never speak to me again," Clara finished the tale on another sigh.

A tap sounded at the door. Upon Mrs. Norgaard's "Yes?" Mrs. Hanson stuck her head in. "There's a young man down here who wants to talk with Clara."

"See, I knew Dag has more sense than you give him credit for."

"No, I don't want to see him. Tell him I'm ill."

"You don't look so good, that's true." Mrs. Hanson withdrew her head and they could hear her thumping down the stairs. Silence settled back in the room.

"You have to see him again."

"I know. But not like this." Clara listened to the silence again. By now, peace had begun it's gentle attack on her strident emotions.

"You know what I think?"

"No, what?"

"I think I see God's hand in all of this and He has a marvelous plan still to be worked out. But not all tonight."

The older woman rose from her chair. "Would you care for a bit of soup or toast?" When Clara shook her head, Mrs. Norgaard just nodded. "All right then, let's get you into bed. Like the Thirtieth Psalm says, 'Weeping may endure for a night, but joy cometh in the morning.' And we want that morning to come soon."

Even after being tucked in and kissed on the forehead, Clara felt sure she'd never cut off the voices in her head long enough to sleep. But the next thing she knew, the rising sun tinted the curtains creamy gold.

The first thing she thought of was Jude on his fancy palomino, high-tailing it out of town. You had to admit, it was funny. Like when the horse kept jumping around. She must have been something when even that big dumb, four-footed beast was scared of her. Anything that would carry Jude around had to be dumb.

She stretched her arms over her head and wriggled her toes. Somewhere a rooster crowed. . .and another answered.

When she thought of Dag, she remembered a dog she'd seen beaten one time. How it crawled away with it's tail dragging in the dirt. Now all his life this man had been beaten on by his conniving younger brother. The fire simmered in her belly again. What could they do to make Jude crawl like the worm he was? How could they get even?

twelve

"I could kill him."

"Dag, no!" Will shook his master's shoulders. "Wake up, Dag, you're dreaming."

Dag fought his way out of the fog and sat upright. He stared at his hands. He could feel his brother's throat clenched between them, his hands squeezing, squeezing the life out. "No!"

"It's all right, come on, everything will be all right." Will murmured in the soothing, singsong voice Dag had taught him to use with a skittish horse. "You'll never kill anyone, not even your brother, even if he does deserve it."

"He was going to use Clara to make a fool out of me again." Dag sank down on the crinkly mattress. "Why does he hate me so? All my life I tried to do as my father said, take care of Ma and my brother. All my life. I know I'm dumb, dolt they called me, and big and ugly, but Will, I tried." He sat up and grasped Will by the collar of his shirt.

"No, Dag, no, no you're not dumb." Will reached for the massive hands of his master and friend.

Dag continued, not even hearing Will's plea. "I quit school so I could go to work and earn some money. They could have farmed but Ma said the land was too poor. Even when I got my own forge, they called me dumb dolt."

"Dag, listen to me. They're just jealous. And lazy and mean."

"Dumb dolt and now I feel such anger I want to kill my brother. My only brother." Dag rolled his head from side to side. After a time he began again. "And now Clara won't see me. After attacking Jude like that. Humph! No one puts anything over on my Clara. God, can't I do anything right?" He threw himself from his bed and thundered out the door of the soddy.

Dag ran as pursued by the devil himself. As his bare feet pounded the mud of the road, his mind kept pace. *God, if You are really the God they talk about in church, take me away from here now. They say there's a heaven. It'd sure beat this life on earth.* He slipped in one viscous hole and fell to his knees. When he rose to run again, he caught himself slipping and sliding with fatigue.

The next time he fell, he lay flat out, face down in the mud. He raised his head just enough to breathe. "God," he panted at the heavens, "I give up! You hear me, I give up!" The words ended on a screech.

Dag lay there waiting for a lightning bolt to strike him. When nothing happened, he pushed himself to his knees and then his feet. When he staggered home, chills rocked his body but he stopped at the windmill and, with one shaking hand, began pumping. After sluicing buckets of clean water and scrubbing with the bar of soap in the scrub bucket, he rinsed again and padded into the soddy. He rubbed himself dry with a coarse towel and fell back in bed. Clean, he finally felt clean. "Father, forgive me," he mumbled as he drifted off to sleep.

The rooster crowing from the farm across the way, brought Dag bolt upright in bed. Had it all been a dream? More like a nightmare. He rubbed the top of his head. No, his hair was still damp. He had indeed lain in the mud and been washed clean. But now he felt. . .he felt like crowing as the rooster did. He began singing instead. "Onward Christian soldiers. . . ." His rich baritone filled the soddy and escaped out the chimney.

Will stumbled from the other room, rubbing his eyes. Dag singing. . .in the morning? Dag singing. . .at all? "Yip-pee!" He dragged his pants from the end of his bed and staggered after Dag, pulling his pants on as he ran.

"I'll go see him as soon as he gets to the shop." Clara took another turn around her room. "He must open at seven." She glanced at the clock on her chest of drawers for the umpteenth time.

"I'll go see her as soon as it is polite." Dag brushed an imaginary piece of straw off his navy wool pants. He gave his hair another brushing.

They met halfway in the middle.

"I'm sorry," they both said at once. They looked at each other and laughed.

"Have you had breakfast?" Clara asked. At the shake of his head, she took his arm. "Good, Mrs. Hanson makes wonderful pancakes."

"I. . .I," they both started to talk again at the same time.

"Ladies first." Dag looked down at the silly black feather bobbing almost at his shoulder. What was she doing wearing such a fancy hat this early in the morning?

"All right. Please forgive me for making such a fool of myself yesterday."

"The only one you made a fool of was my brother. Please, accept my apologies for the way he has acted."

"Of course. Now that that's out of the way, I have a plan. How would you like to get even with your brother? Turn the tables on him for a change?"

"And how would we do this?"

"Well, this way." They climbed the stairs to the porch as she talked. "Jude wanted you to feel like a fool when I learned of his treachery, right?" Dag nodded and opened the door for her. "What if he thought we were courting?"

"How could we do that?" He helped her off with her coat.

"The way everyone courts, silly. You could escort me to church, to the social at the schoolhouse, out for drives in your oh-so-shiny buggy. . . ."

"It's too muddy to take out the buggy." He hung his own coat up.

"Dag, you know what I mean." Together they entered the dining room laughing.

"Now these are the faces I love to see in the morning," Mrs. Norgaard said as she winked at Mrs. Hanson. "I think you better go flip some more of those pancakes of yours and fry extra bacon. Dag looks like he could eat a whole ham."

She turned to the two young people. "Sit down, my children and tell me what brings such smiles to your faces."

"We're going to get even." Clara plunked herself down on her chair. "With Jude. He's been mean to Dag for too long."

A slight frown marred Mrs. Norgaard's forehead. "Get even. You know, God says that is His job."

"I know. But we're going to help Him out." Clara explained the plan, totally seriously and in great detail. "What are you laughing about?"

"I'm not laughing," Mrs. Norgaard swallowed the chortle that belied her words. She sipped her coffee to stifle another giggle. When she had composed her mouth, if not her eyes, she continued. "I think that is a very good plan and you should begin immediately."

Dag looked from his young friend to his old friend and back again. There was something going on here that he could sense but not recognize. But then, how much had he ever tried understanding women in his monastic life anyway? He shrugged the thought away. At least this plan was better than the one he'd dreamed of during the dark hours.

The sun smiled on their plan as they walked through the town that afternoon. Dag recognized one of Jude's cronies standing by the train station so he knew word would get back to his brother. But as he and Clara passed the church, he forgot his brother and remembered the song in his heart when he awoke.

That night he walked with her to their English class at the church. Will accompanied them, hands in his pockets, whistling away. When Dag had shared a little of "the plan" with him, the young man nodded solemnly. "That'll get him for sure," was his only comment. But he didn't stop whistling.

When Dag walked Clara home, Will made excuses and went another way.

"But I don't know how to dance." Dag threw his hands up in the air, hoping to end the discussion.

"But if we are to do this courting right, you must take me to the box social at the schoolhouse on Saturday." Clara sat in the chair in front of the window in the sitting room. Late afternoon sunlight slanted in and set her hair afire.

Dag couldn't take his eyes off the golden threads.

"It's for a good cause. They are trying to earn enough money for a new roof." Clara laid her hands in her lap.

"I'll put the roof on myself," Dag muttered in a voice Clara barely heard.

She wet her lips with the tip of her tongue. "You could learn to dance."

"I suppose you would teach me that, too."

"My box will be the best tasting and prettiest there."

"Will and I do just fine at home. We aren't starving."

"Maybe Jude will be there. This is a perfect opportunity to—"

"Get even. Yes, I know." Dag dragged his hands over his scalp, mussing the hair he usually kept so carefully brushed. "All right. We will go. But we might leave early."

But they didn't leave early and even though Jude never made an appearance, Dag and Clara had a wondrous time. Dag was blessed with the natural rhythm and grace sometimes given to big men and once he learned the patterns of a dance or two, he couldn't get enough. He danced every dance, even those he didn't know.

He danced the waltz with Mrs. Norgaard and the polka with Mrs. Hanson. His feet tapped out the reel with Clara and they swung past each other on the round and square dances. If he made a mistake, he just laughed along with the others and went on dancing.

Clara sank down on a chair along the wall, next to Mrs. Norgaard. "I'm exhausted." She fanned her hot face with her handkerchief. She watched Dag swing Ingeborge past on another polka.

"I think we are seeing a miracle," Mrs. Norgaard whispered in Clara's ear.

"Dag?"

"Yes, Dag. I thank the good Lord every night for what He is doing with our young man."

"I wish. . . ." Clara fanned herself again.

"What, my dear?"

"Oh, nothing. Would you like some punch?" At Mrs. Norgaard's nod, Clara pushed herself to her feet. What she wished was that Dag was truly her young man and that this courting wasn't just a sham.

"Think yer purty smart, don'cha." Jude strolled into the

blacksmith's shop late one afternoon.

Dag ignored him, continuing to forge the point on a pick axe.

"Well, she ain't for the likes a you." Jude spit a glob of tobacco juice into the dirt. "You taken her out to see Ma?"

Dag thrust the heavy steel back into the forge and motioned Will to crank the handle on the blower. The whine of the machine over-powered any conversation. When the iron point glowed red, then white, Dag pulled it out and returned it to the anvil.

"Maybe I shoulda taken that little filly fer m'self after all."

"You have a wife."

"Don't remind me." Jude dug a kerchief out of his back pocket and blew his nose. "We're livin' out at Ma's now. To help her out some'at."

Dag returned the piece of steel to the forge. When he looked up, Jude was gone. Now he'd have to send more food and coal out there. He gritted his teeth and wiped the sweat off his brow with the back of his glove.

Knowing he would have a massive cleaning job afterward, Dag took the surrey out on a Sunday morning to drive the household of women to church. Mrs. Norgaard still wasn't strong enough to walk the distance. When spring came to North Dakota, the frozen roads bottomed out with the thaw, but the streets in town weren't quite the morass of the country roads.

After greeting friends, they entered the sanctuary and

sat side by side. Sharing the same hymn book made them smile at each other. Singing together, her soprano blending with his baritone, made them smile.

Reverend Moen took his place behind the carved, white-and-gilt pulpit. He smiled at those before him. "Grace and peace from God our Father and our Lord Jesus Christ."

Clara settled back against the wooden pew. Today she could truly sense both the grace and peace. She felt it warm her from the inside out. She ignored the warmth emanating from the man beside her and concentrated on the sermon.

"Todays's Gospel is from the Fifth Chapter of Matthew, verse forty-three and following." He glanced again around the congregation and began reading. "'Ye have heard that it hath been said, Thou shalt love thy neighbor, and hate thine enemy. But I say unto you, Love your enemies, bless them that curse you, do good to them that hate you, and pray for them which despitefully use you, and persecute you; That ye may be the children of your Father which is in heaven: for he maketh his sun to rise on the evil and on

the good, and sendeth rain on the just and on the unjust.'"

He closed the Bible and then his eyes. "Father, teach us this day what You would have us to learn. Open our hearts and minds that we might indeed listen unto You. Amen."

The congregation responded with one voice, "Amen."

Clara argued with the verses through the rest of the sermon, only catching random phrases of Reverend Moen's message. *But I have been praying for him, from way back* *when I first received the letter. And right up until. . . ,*she tried a different tack. *I don't hate Jude. . .I. . .I'm just angry with him. Furious is more like it. I don't want to do good to him. . .I want to get even. He hurt Dag, there's no love in the way he has treated Dag all these years.* She groaned inwardly. *Yes, persecute would be the perfect word to describe the way Jude and his mother treated Dag.*

"Our Father so often gives us a promise along with the hard commands, for these words are truly a hard order for us to follow."

Clara covered her unladylike snort with a cough.

"Just think, that we may be children of our Father Who is in Heaven, but Who loved us so much He sent His Son to be persecuted and to die on the cross. . .for you. . .and for me." Reverend Moen leaned forward. There was not a sound from the congregation.

"He forgave each of us. . . ." The pause stretched.

Clara's heart felt like it was being pulled in two directions and at any moment, it might rip in two.

The pastor continued, "And so must we forgive. Amen."

Dag kept his shoulders rigid through super-human efforts. *Forgive! He'd been forgiving them all his life. So they had hurt him. That wasn't so bad, he got used to it. But now Jude had hurt Clara. Beautiful, innocent Clara, whom he hadn't even known. All to play a trick on his ugly dolt of a brother. That he couldn't forgive!*

"As you were forgiven." The words chased each other through his mind and around his heart, stabbing him as they ran.

Am I really a child of God? He looked up at the shiny gold cross in front of the picture of Jesus tending his sheep. Dag stifled a groan that tore from his innermost hidden places.

"He died on the cross. . .for you. . .and for me."

For me. For Dag Weinlander. Dag swallowed hard against the moisture rising in his throat and blinding his eyes. He blinked furiously.

"Our closing hymn for today is Number 360, *My Jesus, I Love Thee.*"

As the organ wheezed into the opening bars of the song, Clara and Dag stood along with the congregation. The words poured forth. "My Jesus, I love thee, I know thou art mine. For thee all the folly of sin I resign. . . ."

Dag quit singing. He bit his lip and let the words and music roll over him, bathing him in the healing Christ promised. He whispered along with the final line. "If ever I loved thee, my Jesus 'tis now."

Clara struggled to reach the high notes—and gave up. Singing was impossible from a throat clogged with tears. Why did Reverend Moen choose such a sermon for today? Had someone told him about their game? Who would? And was it *really* a game? Was getting even ever a game?

Neither Dag nor Clara spoke a word on the ride home, until they arrived at the big house and then it was only a polite goodbye.

The doorbell announced a visitor just as the grandfather's clock bonged six times.

"Come right on in," Mrs. Hanson said. "You're just in

time for supper."

"No, I mean, no thank you. I'd just like a few minutes with Clara, if I may." Dag gripped his hat in his hands. This would be the hardest thing he'd ever done.

When Clara came to the door, he stared into her eyes, then dropped his gaze to the floor. "Could you come out for a moment please?"

She nodded, reached behind her for the shawl on the coat tree and stepped outside, her gaze never leaving his face. "What is it, Dag. What's wrong?"

Her soft voice tore his heart from his chest. "I. . .we . . .that is, I cannot play our courting game any longer." He took a deep breath. "And I cannot see you anymore." He turned and stepped off the porch, his long strides eating up the distance to the fence.

"Dag, what is it?"

He kept on walking.

Clara chewed on her knuckle for one brief moment and flew down the walk after him. When he didn't stop at her calling his name, she grabbed his coat when she caught him.

"Now, tell me what this is all about." She put all the force she could into her words.

"*Nei*, no. Just let it be."

"Dag, you can't run away from me now. Not now or anytime." Clara grasped his lapels with shaking hands. "You can't leave because I love you and you love me if you'd just open your eyes. If you can't see it, maybe I should take one of your hammers and smack you over the head with it till you get some sense."

"You love me?" His voice squeaked.

Clara stepped back. She tipped her head slightly to the side and glared up at him. "I said so, didn't I?"

Dag grabbed her around the waist with both hands and whirled them both around. "She loves me," he yelled to the robin who fluttered out of his nighttime perch at all the commotion.

He set her down just long enough to wrap both arms around her and lifting her for the kiss he'd dreamed of during the long winter nights.

Clara wrapped her arms around his neck and kissed him back. When they drew apart to breathe, she traced one slim fingertip across his full bottom lip. "I like kissing a man with a beard," she whispered and placed her lips on his again. "But only if that man is you." Her breathy voice tickled the soft hairs around his mouth.

Slowly, he set her down, never letting her move from the circle of his arms. "I feel like Jacob who stole the birthright," he confessed.

"No, you have it backwards. "You're the older. Your brother has spent most of his life trying to steal the birthright from you. But now you know how much you are worth. And nothing, no one, can take that or me from you."

"Clara, my heart, I love you." There, he'd said the words. He couldn't remember ever uttering them before. Such simple words. He thought back to this morning. He had said them before. Today, in church. Only it was a different love song, "My Jesus, I love thee, I know thou art mine." He looked deep into Clara's eyes, searching her soul. "My Clara, I love thee, I know thou art mine." And thus he gave her his heart.

epilogue

Clara rocked gently in the chair on the wide front porch. She could hear the canary singing from Mrs. Norgaard's room up above. He serenaded them from the first rays of sunlight until the golden ball sank in the west.

On the flagpole attached to the house, she could hear the Norwegian flag fluttering in the breeze. The seventeeth of May, Norwegian Independence Day and Clara and Dag's one year anniversary.

She leaned her head against the back of the seat and closed her eyes. What a day that had been. No, to be exact, the celebration had begun the week before that when Mrs. Norgaard called her and Dag into the sitting room one evening.

After they took their places on the brown velvet couch, a gentle silence permeated the room.

"I have something for you," she said, her face serious but her eyes sending messages of warmth and love. "I've put off telling you this because I don't want you to be burdened by an old woman's silliness."

"What is it?" Clara felt alarm leaping in her heart. Was something wrong with her friend? Something she'd not told them?

Mrs. Norgaard leaned forward and handed them an

183

envelope. When Clara looked up in consternation, the old woman just nodded.

Dag slit the envelope open and removed a parchment sheet. Together, he and Clara read the formal words.

Clara felt her mouth fall open. She stared from the letter to Mrs. Norgaard and back to the paper in Dag's hands. "You mean, you. . . ?" She couldn't get the rest of the words out.

"Yes, the house is yours, but only if you truly want it."

"Want it? How could you doubt something so wonderful?"

"But that means you will be burdened with me until the good Lord calls me home."

"No, not a burden." Dag shook his head. "You have given me a life." He clasped Clara's hand in his own. "And a wife, and now a home."

"Then I believe we have made a fair trade for without Clara, I would not be here to rejoice with you." Mrs. Norgaard blinked rapidly, matching the motions of the two on the settee.

Clara crossed the small space and dropped to her knees in front of her mentor. "Thank you, from the bottom of my heart."

Mrs. Norgaard stroked back the tendrils of silky hair that framed Clara's face. "I have one more favor to ask."

"What? Anything."

"Just fill these rooms with laughing children as soon as you can, so I can enjoy them, too."

Clara, dreaming in the rocker, stroked her rounded

belly. Little Lars or Lisa seemed in a mighty big hurry to make their entrance or else they were practicing broad jumps.

She sighed. And the wedding had been magnificent. Her in her *bunad* and Nora in hers. Now neither of them would fit into their black skirts or sparkling aprons. Their babies would be born close together.

Dag had stood before the congregation after the pronouncement of man and wife. "I have something I'd like to say," he announced. He glanced at Reverend Moen for permission. At the preacher's nod, Dag continued. "Most of you knew me long before Clara came to Soldall. You brought your plowshares to be sharpened and your horses to be shod. But I was not one to talk and share the latest news."

A ripple of laughter spread across the congregation.

"But you saw me then and you see me now. What happened to me was God's miracle. He took a bitter, beaten man and poured love into his heart, that love that Christ talks about. God used a young woman to bring life to many of us in this town and then He gave her to me. Can you doubt God's great love? If He could love me, He can love anyone."

There wasn't a dry eye in the place.

Clara straightened from her idyll on the porch. The familiar whistle announced the arrival of her beloved whistler. She watched through the breaks in the newly leafed trees for glimpses of his head as he strode the street for home. She rubbed her back again.

Dag took the porch steps in one bound. "Have you been resting like you were told?" he asked, his smile causing her heart to leap in response.

"I have. Resting and remembering." She laid her cheek against the back of his hand.

"Remembering?"

"Oh, about the wedding and the months before that." She kissed a spot on his hand that had gotten too close to the heat.

Dag sank down on the floor beside her, one arm propped on a raised knee. "I have a confession to make."

Clara's eyebrows traveled upward.

"Your present didn't come in on the train."

Clara rubbed her back again and this time squirmed a bit in the seat. "I think yours might be coming sooner than we expected."

Dag turned in time to catch a grimace mar the serenity of her forehead. "Are you all right?" A hint of panic touched his voice.

"I'm fine. Or I will be after a few more hours." She stroked her fingers through the coffee-hued hair that waved back so richly from his face. She'd come to Dakota to find her dream and now they were living it.

A Letter To Our Readers

Dear Reader:

In order that we might better contribute to your reading enjoyment, we would appreciate your taking a few minutes to respond to the following questions. When completed, please return to the following:

Karen Carroll, Editor
Heartsong Presents
P.O. Box 719
Uhrichsville, Ohio 44683

1. Did you enjoy reading *Dakota Dream*?
   ☐ Very much. I would like to see more books
      by this author!
   ☐ Moderately
      I would have enjoyed it more if _____

   _____

2. Are you a member of *Heartsong Presents*? Yes   No
   If no, where did you purchase this book? _____

   _____

3. What influenced your decision to purchase
   this book? (Circle those that apply.)

Cover	Back cover copy
Title	Friends
Publicity	Other _____

4. On a scale from 1 (poor) to 10 (superior), please rate the following elements.

    ___Heroine   ___Plot

    ___Hero   ___Inspirational theme

    ___Setting   ___Secondary characters

5. What settings would you like to see covered in *Heartsong Presents* books?

_____

_____

6. What are some inspirational themes you would like to see treated in future books?_____

_____

_____

7. Would you be interested in reading other *Heartsong Presents* titles?   Yes   No

8. Please circle your age range:
Under 18   18-24   25-34
35-45   46-55   Over 55

9. How many hours per week do you read? _____

Name _____

Occupation _____

Address _____

City _____ State _____ Zip _____

add a little *MYSTERY* to your romance!

TWO GREAT INSPIRATIONAL ROMANCES
WITH JUST A TOUCH OF MYSTERY
BY MARLENE J. CHASE

_____*The Other Side of Silence*—Anna Durham finds a purpose for living in the eyes of a needy child and a reason to love in the eyes of a lonely physician...but first the silence of secrets must be broken. HP6 BHSB-07 $2.95.

_____*This Trembling Cup*—A respite on a plush Wisconsin resort may just be the thing for Angie Carlson's burn-out—or just the beginning of a devious plot unraveling and the promise of love. HP5 BHSB-05 $2.95.